Desmond Cory (a p
ing, Sussex. He se
Marines before go
Peter's College, Ox
for a while, ending
wife. On his retu
English for seventeen
in the Middle East.

He now lives and works in Cyprus, and when not writing books likes to play golf and to travel.

DESMOND CORY

The Strange Attractor

PAN BOOKS
in association with Macmillan London

First published 1991 by Macmillan London Ltd
This edition first published 1992 by Pan Books Ltd
Cavaye Place, London SW10 9PG
in association with Macmillan London Ltd
1 3 5 7 9 8 6 4 2

ISBN 0 330 31938 8

Printed in England by Clays Ltd, St Ives plc

1

'Too bad about Cantwell, isn't it?'

'Um,' Dobie said.

He wondered who the hell Cantwell was. Probably someone who'd strained his knee before the Test Match, or developed a blister on his spinning finger. Dobie disliked being forced to admit his ignorance on such topics of universal interest as this, so, 'Um,' he said.

'Tragedy, really,' said Merrick, dipping his long nose into a plastic teacup.

Merrick, though, Dobie thought, struggling to emerge from the mood of misty somnolence in which he usually passed the eleven o'clock coffee-break. It wouldn't be cricket, then. Mervyn Evans was cricket. Merrick didn't know a bloody thing about cricket. Merrick didn't know a bloody thing about anything except Mackintosh computers. Could Cantwell conceivably be a . . . ? Surely not. Even though they gave them such extraordinary names nowadays. 'What exactly, er . . . happened?'

'I thought you knew,' Merrick said. 'He shot himself.'

Dobie felt instantly relieved. Cantwell, then, was definitely not a computer but some form or other of the human species. That still left the field pretty wide open. His demise was, however, at least in Merrick's view, a tragedy. It really sounded very much like a student. Or a member of the staff. Though in the latter case, one would have expected Merrick to sound a little more pleased about it.

Either way, it seemed the sort of thing about which he, Dobie, should really have been informed by someone or other. It was disgraceful. 'No one tells me anything these days,' Dobie said somewhat plaintively. 'It's disgraceful. Shot himself? Good heavens.'

'Well, you wouldn't want to go round shouting about it from the rooftops.'

'What a peculiar suggestion, Gwyn. Nothing could have been further from my mind.'

'What I *mean*,' said Merrick patiently, 'is that we don't want to give the impression that our graduates have formed the habit of shooting themselves as soon as they've gone into business. It discourages prospective employers.'

'Graduates? There've been other cases, then?'

'No, no. Not that I know of. I used the plural form merely to establish my point.'

'I see.' Dobie considered the matter for a moment. 'Which was . . . ?'

'Well, that's why you mightn't have been told about it, is all.'

'No question of *mightn't*, Gwyn. I wasn't, I most definitely wasn't.'

'Neither was I, if it comes to that. There was a bit about it in the paper.'

'Ah. Poor chap.' Cantwell? 'Poor chap.' *Cantwell?* . . . No. No bell rang. 'When did it happen?'

'Day before yesterday. We were talking about it earlier, but you couldn't have been listening.'

This was highly probable. Dobie glanced at his wrist-watch and hurriedly drank what was left of his tea. It was almost cold. Borrodaile and Wain, he now saw, had left the room already. Annoying. He had wanted to have a word with Wain about something or other. 'In business, you said?'

'Eh?'

'Who was he working for?'

'Corder Acoustics,' Merrick said. 'Doing well, too, from all accounts.'

'Some private problem, then.'

'One has to suppose so.'

'Ah well. Life must go on. Papers to mark.'

'Back to the grind,' Merrick agreed. Unenthusiastically. 'Still, only two more weeks down the tube, thank heaven.'

Dobie, having mentally checked the mathematical verifiability of this assertion and determined it to be correct to four decimal places, nodded, placed his empty cup on the windowsill, picked up his briefcase and made for the door, discovering when halfway there that the briefcase was someone else's. It wasn't the first time this had happened. He would have to find out who the other briefcase belonged to and complain about it. Have it painted white, or something. He returned to effect the needed substitution, then wandered through the door obscurely marked

STA F ROOM
DEPT ATH MATI S

and turned to the left down the corridor. Merrick had already disappeared from sight, and a faint but penetrating drone from the rooms to either side indicated that the third teaching session of the morning was under way. In other words, Dobie was late, as usual. He paused and lit a cigarette to show how little he cared. The door to his right was a fraction ajar and a persuasively well-modulated voice, recognisable as Borrodaile's, emerged from it.

'. . . now the image or if you prefer it the figure that we have on the board representing our average ratio of persistence it's evident that developments will be demonstrated by variations or fluctuations ascending or descending the level of our original curve and you'll also have observed that our average ratio will remain at par in spite of such variations as may take place in the comparative prices of the basic commodities that have been taken into account and this is because of the precisely analogous movement in an opposite direction of the prices of related or residual commodities through which the ascent or descent of our curve must be cancelled out. Therefore, in order to establish an equation expressing the stimulation–depression ratio in the production of a given commodity . . .'

The voice faded to insignificance as Dobie moved down the corridor. It was interesting, and sometimes encouraging, to overhear other people's lectures; Dobie was sincere in his belief that his own expositions came close to establishing what might be called a maximum of incomprehensibility, but the evidence was incontrovertible that others pressed hard on his heels. Certainly the average stimulation–depression ratio strongly favoured the latter. The final equation would thus represent a total ellipse, its centre lying at the point of origin. That, Dobie thought, sighing like a meditative grampus as he turned the corner, is the trouble with me. My major axis is horizontal, and I'm living on a world with an equinox. That has to be why I'm five minutes late for all my lectures.

Eight minutes late, today.

He set his foot on his half-smoked cigarette and entered Room 449. This was one of the pleasanter rooms in the Old Building, overlooking Cathays Park; you could see the lawns from the lecturer's dais but not from the students' desks. The desks were currently occupied by Physics III, who were aware of the social injustice of this arrangement and tended rather to shuffle. They became relatively quiet, however, on Dobie's entrance, and as he sat down converted themselves from fourteen individuals into the usual communal entity, rather as a group of wandering wolves might convert themselves, on scenting a passing elk, into a pack. Dobie opened his briefcase.

'Today,' he said, 'I'm going to explain to you some of the difficulties of expressing complex numbers in trigonometric form.'

Goody, goody. The ethos of the class became miasmic with vague recollection; the pages of textbooks were agitatedly fluttered, and Hywel Morgan opened his large black box of geometrical instruments. 'I shall want,' Dobie said, 'to refer specifically to de Moivre's theorem, so first of all let's refresh our memories. We'll multiply two complex numbers together and we'll have them both expressed in trigonometric form . . .'

Voices were resounding all through the Old Building. Another had been added to their number. That was all.

Dobie in fact had certain memories that didn't need to be refreshed and which at times affected his concentration if not the flow of his discourse. Most of them concerned his wife Jenny and an ex-student of his called Mike Frascati who ran the BMW agency somewhere down the Newport Road. Mike hadn't been a very good student but he was probably a very good car salesman and as such pulled in something like three times Dobie's salary, to say nothing of the odd perks – which spectacularly included one of those low-slung silver-sprayed snarly monstrosities elaborately festooned in exhaust pipes in which, on more than one occasion, Dobie, driving sedately homewards in his unassuming Ford Fiesta, had passed him, though going in the opposite direction, naturally. (The idea of passing a thing like that would in any other circumstances have struck him as both laughable and absurd.) Dobie had been animated at the time by the vague hope that if he kept *very* still the nasty dog sniffing at his trouser-legs would go away, having first pissed all over his boots, and that was more or less what had happened. Mike, at any rate, had been transferred to Birmingham and had been gone a month now. But things hadn't changed in the slightest. *What* things?

Well . . .

Hard to say. Dobie was not inexperienced in these matters himself, having been involved earlier in his career in a liaison with a married woman. Of course, way back in the swinging Seventies it had hardly been possible to lean out of a window and heave a brick without hitting some fellow or other who was, had been or else was about to be in Dobie's present position precisely, unless by great good luck you hit his wife instead. Dobie's lady friend of the time (whose name now momentarily escaped him) had undoubtedly taken up adultery in the way she might have taken up yoga or basket-weaving or flower-arranging; obediently in accordance with *l'esprit du temps* and the recommendations of the Sunday supplements they had tied themselves into strenuous and complicated knots in the backs of motor-cars, in the unfrequented parts of golf courses and so forth, while also feeling themselves free – not to say obscurely compelled – in the privacy of Dobie's own small flat to do it not only on the bed, in the old-fashioned way, but also on the sofa, on the sitting-room carpet (accompanied by the London Symphony Orchestra playing Mozart's twenty-ninth) and even, on one memorable occasion, on top of the kitchen table (the occasion being memorable because the legs of the table had proved inadequate to it, the resultant repair bill totalling an exorbitant seven pounds twenty, plus the price of a bottle of iodine and elastoplast). They had even attended the showing of a number of glum Scandinavian films, where Dobie's desperate efforts simultaneously to absorb the visual content and to read the sub-titles had caused him to leave the cinema cross-eyed, and had together perused a somewhat esoteric book which told you about things to do with electric light bulbs, only you couldn't because you needed the electric light bulb to read the book by (an interesting application, as Dobie had then noted, of Heisenberg's uncertainty principle). Dobie, in short, had been *through* all that.

But whatever Jenny was going through, it wasn't like that at all.

Ceasing to muse sadly upon the dear departed days of his full and entertaining sex life, Dobie pushed open the door of his flat – yes, still the same small flat – and went in. At once he heard his wife's voice upraised in song, cheerfully trilling some outdated number vaguely to be associated with Fred Astaire and Ginger what's-her-name. Off key, of course. *That* was one of the things. She was always *singing*. This time her voice was emanating from the bedroom. Dobie plonked down his briefcase where it always went, on the small table in the narrow hallway, and peered round the half-open door. 'Oh, it's you,' he said.

Jenny had short black hair and she was sitting in front of the dressing-table mirror, brushing it. She seemed disposed to treat this remark with a merited contempt. 'Who else would it be?'

'I mean, you're not out,' Dobie explained. 'You're in.'

'Looks like it,' Jenny said. 'How'd the exams go?'

'I was lecturing today.'

'Ah.'

Dobie found her quite often in the bedroom. It was arguably the nicest room in the flat, or anyway the only one with any kind of a view. The view was of the carport outside and of a few sheltering trees, but it was better than nothing. And there were French windows, open now to the summer air, giving on to a balcony from where you got exactly the same view, this being a ground-floor flat. 'Well, I'm going out this evening,' Jenny said. 'Jane phoned. So you can get on with your marking.'

'Ah,' Dobie said.

Papers to mark. Quite so. He went back to pick up his briefcase and went through the sitting-room to his study. So-called. Not a sparkling conversation, that, but characteristic.

To be fair, he hadn't married Jenny because of her conversational prowess. These days it was difficult to remember why he *had* married her, really. Or why she'd married him. Though in his case no doubt a normal concupiscence had played its part. A holiday affair, you could say, that had got out of hand. Dobie wasn't very good at taking holidays and there it was. Last year he'd tried one of those package things on the Côte d'Azur and after the usual never-agains he'd run into Jenny or more exactly into Jenny's bikini and had changed his mind. Jenny had been the travel agency courier and, Dobie's French being rudimentary, had been useful to him in all kinds of ways. Of course nearly *all* the women at the hotel had worn bikinis round the pool but Jenny had been twenty years younger than they were and you couldn't really . . . Quite. She was also twenty years younger than *he* was but that hadn't seemed to matter at the time. Or now, for that matter. *That* wasn't the problem. Or he didn't think so.

Dobie seated himself in his revolving chair and stared for a while at Eddie. Eddie was good at problems. *Some private problem, then? One has to suppose so*. Obviously Cantwell had had a few. Dobie found it difficult, though, to imagine the kind of problems that might cause a promising young lad of twenty-something to pick up a gun and fire it the wrong way round. Smith and Wesson's cure for insomnia. Yes. Most amusing.

He still couldn't remember what Cantwell looked like. Or *had* looked like. And that was annoying. He addressed himself to Eddie's keyboard and rattled out the necessary instructions. Eddie hurriedly searched for Cantwell and found him almost at once.

CANTWELL SJ 21043
ELEC ENG 1986
SUPERVISOR DJ MARRYAT

The record was on file, anyway. Dobie typed

CHECK FINAL C/A FIGURES

and waited for Eddie to come up with the goods. Eddie barely hesitated.

MATHS	92
ENG DRAWING	74
MECH TECH	70
PHYSICS	84
ELEC ENG	68
APP THERMO	65
ELEC MACHINERY	71

Eddie didn't need to supply the average figure; Dobie could work that out in his head and almost as fast. It was pretty commendable. That 92 for Maths would have been on Wain's marking but even so. Anyone coming up with a final year 92 had to be a mathematician of a kind; someone whose cerebral processes might be different to Dobie's own but in no way radically dissimilar. Of course, they were now. It was puzzling.

Feeling the need for a caffeine stimulant, Dobie switched off Eddie and switched on the electric kettle in the kitchen instead. Jenny, as was evident, had taken her lunch in the kitchen and the table was strewn with cracker crumbs and liberally anointed with smears of peanut butter. Jenny was *addicted* to peanut butter. Dobie, who was fast becoming addicted to clearing up after her, did so while the kettle boiled. Afterwards and bearing his steaming mug he wandered back into the bedroom, where Jenny was donning various of her glad rags preparatory to going out. Somewhere.

'It seems,' Dobie said, 'one of my ex-students has committed suicide.'

'Really?' Jenny said, adjusting the fit of her skirt in the wardrobe mirror. 'How awful.'

'Shot himself. Or so they tell me.'

'That's awful,' Jenny said again, in so abstracted a tone that Dobie wasn't sure if she were alluding to the fatality or to her hemline. 'Did I know him?'

'I don't think so. Name of Cantwell. He graduated last year.'

'Don't remember.'

'To be honest,' Dobie said, 'nor do I.'

He placed his coffee mug on the side table where Jenny did a very occasional spot of typing and sat down alongside. The bed would have been more comfortable but was now monopolised by Jenny's discarded clothing. 'He'd have been quite young, I suppose,' Jenny said. 'Terrible for his parents. But there's not much *you* can do about it, is there?'

'No. There isn't.'

'Well, I won't be late. Eight o'clockish.'

She threw her jacket over one shoulder, picked up her bag and went out. Dobie heard the click of the front door closing and drank more coffee. The view from where he sat presently included the side elevation of her lemon-yellow Mini parked in the carport beside the rather dustier Fiesta; Dobie watched her enter it, slamming the door behind her, fuss for a moment or two with the driving mirror and then start the motor, reversing the Mini neatly round the corner and out of sight. It looked like a fine summer evening out there. Dobie debated with himself whether or not to go out for a short stroll round the park, deciding in the end against it.

He had papers to mark.

* * *

'Who's Mr Marryat?'

'Oh *him*, then,' said Mrs Hart. She hit the shift key a spiteful wallop and typed another line all in capitals.

'New, isn't he?'

'That depends on what you mean by *new*.'

'I don't think I know him,' Dobie said patiently. Mrs Hart was herself an old stager by any manner of reckoning, having been secretary to the Head of Electrical for the past fifteen years or more. That gave her an unofficial ranking of somewhere round Senior Lecturer status; diplomacy, therefore, paid or was anyway prudent.

'Ooooooo,' Mrs Hart said. 'Not everyone does.'

'But *you* do, don't you?'

'He'll have been here now for a couple of years, all told. He's one of *those*, you know.'

This expression, so fraught with significance in non-collegiate circles, had other connotations in its present context and Dobie was able to decipher its meaning, though only just. '. . . industrial?'

'Davies, Parry and Kendrick. Over to Bristol.'

'Arrrrr.'

'Very up-and-coming firm they are. And we have their Mr Marryat with us on a research readership, that's how it is.'

'So how would I be able to get hold of him?'

'He shares a room with Dr Mankowitz in the Tower Block. Number 22. Would you care for me to call on the telephone and see if he's there?'

'No, no,' Dobie said. 'Don't bother. I have to go round there anyway.'

This last was not strictly true, but Dobie was thoroughly familiar with that Law of Premeditated Motion whereby a college lecturer whose whereabouts have been established by telephone will be deemed to have taken the necessary steps to establish himself elsewhere by the time one has arrived at the place where he was before, the application of this law being facilitated by the fact that it is impossible to move from one point to another in a modern college building without surmounting at least three flights of stairs. Dobie arrived outside room 22 in his usual state of mild breathlessness and knocked at the door. 'Come in,' somebody said.

The room was full, like all the others in the block, of desks and filing cabinets composed of a shiny plastic material. These had been introduced into staff quarters the previous year to give the correct impression of modern design and hi-tech executive efficiency; since then, however, they – like all the others in the block – had been totally buried under piles of mouldering papers, exam scripts, folders, ashtrays, matchboxes, envelopes, biscuit tins and daily newspapers left open at the racing results and there forgotten. There remained just sufficient space for two metal-backed chairs into which their respective owners might ease themselves, the heaps of decaying matter behind which they then virtually disappeared being thus, so to speak, held at bay and forced to mould themselves around the seated person's outline. Marryat's outline was an exceptionally long and thin one – one that gave the accumulated junk a good deal of encouragement. The encroaching jungle seemed to be about to strike, to wipe him out entirely; at any moment he might disappear and civilisation be routed. 'Come in,' he said again, this time with a touch of irritation.

'I *am* in,' Dobie said.

Marryat's visage thereupon came briefly into view, like Paul Gauguin peering out from between the palm leaves. 'So you are. So you are. Mr Forbes, I think?'

'No, my name's Dobie. Mathematics.'

'Ah yes. Professor Dobie. I knew the face was familiar but—' Marryat took off his glasses and rubbed his eyes.

'I wondered,' Dobie said, 'if you could spare me

a moment. About a student. An ex-student, rather.'

'Oh yes. Of course. Do make yourself at home.'

Dobie cleared a space on the edge of the desk with the casual expertise of long practice, his own over-crowded rabbit-hutch being almost identical to this one, and perched his behind precariously upon it. 'Cantwell.'

'Ah, Cantwell.' Marryat put his glasses back on. 'Sad business, that.'

'I understand you were his supervisor when he was up.'

'So I was, so I was. A very sad business indeed.'

'And since then he's been working for Corder Acoustics.'

'Yes, that's correct.'

'Did you visit him there? I mean, in the normal run of events—'

'Oh yes. Through the settling-in period. Just checking up on how things were going. The usual thing.'

'And how *were* they going?'

'No complaints. In fact, very much the contrary. He seemed to be enjoying his work. And giving every satisfaction, they told me.'

'Doing what?'

'D and R. Design and Research Section.'

'And he liked the job?'

'He certainly seemed to.'

'So what was his problem?'

'Problem?' Marryat scratched the tip of his nose. 'Ah. I see what you mean. I haven't a clue. He may have left a note or something, I understand that's what they often . . . Anyway, they're holding the inquest this afternoon and I expect the facts will come out, it's to be supposed they will. After all, that's what inquests are for.'

'Are you attending?'

'Not officially,' Marryat said. 'No, *I* shan't go. I can't get away and in any case—'

'Why should you?'

'Exactly. You haven't any . . . special interest in him, have you?'

'You might say a personal interest.'

'Did you?'

'Did I what?'

'Say that.'

'Say what?'

'That you had a personal interest.'

'I would have done if you'd asked me but you didn't.'

'Didn't what?'

'Ask me if I had a personal interest.'

Marryat, who was not so used to this kind of a conversation as were Dobie's more immediate colleagues, took off his glasses once again and began to rub them very hard with a very clean handkerchief. 'I didn't mean if you'd said it to *me*,' he said, knocking over a box file with his elbow. Spilled papers added themselves to the variegated débris on the floor. 'It doesn't really matter what I meant, anyhow. I think I've forgotten. Dickie Bird is the chap you ought to see. That's if you want to see anyone.'

'About what?'

Marryat rubbed harder than ever. 'About Cantwell's work. He's the Head of Section.'

'He'll be at the inquest, then?'

'I should think it probable.'

'And there'll be medical evidence and so forth.'

'I believe that's customary.'

The medical evidence was given by an outwardly rather formidable dark-haired young lady called Dr Coyle and Dobie didn't understand very much of it. He hadn't expected to. However, the coroner, a not at all formidable man with a red nose and matching moustache, seemed to be in no way fazed and made copious notes.

Dobie had never attended an inquest before and wasn't very impressed. The room was small and poorly lit and remarkably sparsely populated. Only eight other persons, including the coroner, appeared to be present and Dobie didn't recognise any of them. It all compared very unfavourably with the ones he'd seen on the telly, with Lord Peter Wimsey in the box or whatever it was called. It didn't much matter what it was called because there wasn't one. Dr Coyle had given her evidence sitting on a hard wooden chair at the table opposite the coroner and having given it was still sitting there, hands folded patiently in her lap. While the coroner went on scribbling away. The whole show was decidedly lacking in zip.

'Dr Coyle,' the coroner said, eventually. 'Besides having performed the pathological examination, and I thank you for reporting upon it so cogently . . . you in fact discovered the body?'

'I did,' Dr Coyle said. In a high, clear and perhaps excessively ladylike voice, suggestive of Meryl Streep in one of her Mayfair-scrubber routines.

'You were in fact personally acquainted with the deceased? And you indeed carried out the formal identification of the body at Detective-Inspector Jackson's request?'

'Yes, I was. And yes, I did.'

'So what was your exact relationship with Mr Cantwell?'

'I was his landlady.'

Somebody at the back sniffed penetratingly. The coroner put down his pencil. 'Would you amplify on that?'

'Certainly. He rented a first-floor bedsitter and kitchenette. He'd lived there these past three years. The other first-floor rooms I use myself. The ground floor is where I have my clinic.'

'This is at 12 Ludlow Road?'

'Yes.'

The coroner drew a sheet of paper from under his notebook and studied it cautiously. 'Yes. I have a sketch-map here which makes the layout of the premises fairly clear. Now, as to your discovery of the body . . . ?'

'I conducted my morning clinic just as usual, finished just after twelve thirty and went upstairs to make some coffee. About ten minutes later I went into Sammy's, that's Mr Cantwell's room—'

'For what purpose?'

'I wanted to steal some sugar.'

'Ah. On nefarious intent.'

'Yes,' Dr Coyle said. She didn't smile. 'I assumed he was out at work, which would normally have been the case. But on entering the room I immediately saw the body lying on the floor, face downwards, close to the workdesk. He had a gun in his right hand – an automatic pistol, I believe. There was blood on the rug under his head and clearly visible trauma to the right side of his skull. I made sure that he was dead and then returned to my flat to phone the police. When they arrived, Inspector Jackson asked me to make a fuller examination of the body in my capacity as police pathologist and I did so. I didn't go back to the room until then.'

'But you had previously been there for a space of . . . ?'

'Not more than three minutes.'

Dr Coyle, in point of fact, was not unattractive. Irish-blue eyes, shiny black hair and a high, rounded forehead. She wore, probably for the occasion, what Dobie imagined to be an executive costume, tailor-made and navy blue in colour. The general severity of her appearance didn't suggest, as is sometimes the case, that her air of professional competence was a mere façade; no indeed. This chick was on the ball. The coroner seemed to be well aware of this and to be, if anything, faintly on the defensive. 'And during this time you made a preliminary examination of the body?'

'I also looked quickly around the room to see if there was any kind of letter or suicide note. But there wasn't. Not that I could see.'

'I understand the police haven't found one so I think we can assume that nothing of that nature . . . But obviously, then, your first impression was that Mr Cantwell had shot himself?'

'Yes. That's still my opinion.'

'Quite so.'

'I should add that at that time I didn't touch or disturb anything in the room in any way.'

'I'd rather taken that for granted, Dr Coyle, in view of your experience in these matters. Nothing else struck your notice as being at all unusual?'

'Nothing.'

'The door of the room was unlocked?'

'Yes. It was normally kept locked when Mr Cantwell was out. But on this occasion, of course, he wasn't.'

'As his landlady, you would have had a spare key?'

'That's right. I expected to have to use it.'

'But in the event you didn't have to. Yes. Just to make this point completely clear, you found the door unlocked but closed? Not open or ajar?'

'The door was unlocked but closed.'

'Thank you,' the coroner said. He started writing once again in his notebook. Dobie wondered what all *that* had been about. Throughout the interchange his attention had drifted slightly towards the other occupants of the courtroom; he rather thought he had successfully identified the Corder Acoustics rep as a tall technical gent in rimless glasses and the stocky curly-haired bloke in the regrettable suit would almost certainly be here on behalf of the local fuzz. '. . . You've said that you estimate death to have occurred an hour or so previously? At approximately eleven thirty?'

'That's correct.'

'At which time you were of course conducting your clinic downstairs. We have to take it that you didn't hear the shot? Or any kind of movement or disturbance?'

'Plenty of movement and disturbance. As in any other clinic. But I didn't hear the shot, no. Nor did my receptionist or any of the patients in the waiting-room. If I'd heard anything like that, naturally I'd have investigated.'

The coroner seemed to be examining his sketch-map again. 'I see that Mr Cantwell's room is at the opposite end of the house to your consulting room. That may in part account for it.'

'Yes, and it's a very solid building. With thick walls.'

'Now I'm going to forestall Detective-Inspector Jackson's evidence, Dr Coyle, and ask you if you were able to recognise the gun?'

'I recognised it as being identical or very similar to one that belonged to Mr Cantwell, yes.'

'So you knew that he possessed a gun?'

'He showed it to me once. Also where he kept it. In the chest of drawers, under his shirts.'

Somebody else at the back of the room was also making notes assiduously. An earnest-looking lad in his early twenties, wearing a crumpled sports jacket and a worried expression; a cub reporter from the *Echo*, likely as not. Not much for *him* here, surely? Or for anyone else. Dobie sighed windily. It wasn't as though he had nothing better to do, what with papers to mark, calculations to be checked, Jenny to worry about . . . That peculiar business of the blonde wig, for instance. *There* was a mystery for you. What the hell would she be doing with a *blonde wig*? . . .

'Can you say *why* he kept a gun?'

'He bought it some six months ago with the idea of protecting the premises. You see, the clinic downstairs has been broken into on three separate occasions lately, presumably by people who hoped to find drugs there.

I *do* keep drugs there, of course. Mr Cantwell was worried about my safety because these can be very nasty people. So he got this gun though I think his intention was to threaten these people with it, should the need arise, rather than to use it. I didn't think it was a good idea and I told him so very emphatically.'

'You knew that the gun was unlicensed?'

'I didn't know that because I never asked him. But I certainly assumed that he didn't have a licence for it. I asked him to get rid of it and he later told me that he had. Obviously, that couldn't have been true.'

Lots of women wore wigs. For all Dobie knew, blonde wigs might be trendy. But why be so secretive about it? Why would she think that *he* cared, one way or another? It was all so . . . Yes. Well. Dobie wiggled his behind against his uncomfortable seat and tried to concentrate on the court proceedings. It wasn't easy.

'I understand,' the coroner was saying, 'that the police haven't been able to trace his relatives.'

'No, I couldn't help them there very much. His parents died some years back, or so he told me, in a car accident. In Australia. There was an uncle in London he used to visit occasionally but I don't know the address.'

'Did Mr Cantwell receive many letters? To your knowledge?'

'Very few letters. He didn't write many, either. He didn't like writing letters. He always said he was numerate, not literate.'

'I'm not sure what that means but we'll let it pass. Would you say he was a lonely man?'

'Yes, I think I would.'

'Not many visitors?'

'Again, hardly any. To my knowledge. Though I mightn't know if he had. I have so many professional engagements—'

'Yes, I understand that. Did *you* think of him as a friend, Dr Coyle?'

'Our relationship was perfectly friendly, but I wouldn't say that I *thought* of him as a friend. If I were a more maternal person I'd say my attitude was . . . Well . . .'

'In loco parentis?'

'Not exactly. I suppose I felt sorry for him.'

'Why?'

'I think I've explained why. He didn't have many friends. Nor do I, if it comes to that.'

'Did he have any friends of the opposite sex?'

'None that I know of.'

The coroner gazed upwards at the ceiling. 'I suppose I'm really asking you if you can shed any light on what motives he may have had for taking his own life. Because they're not very evident, on the face of it.'

'I know he had money problems. But I didn't think they were all that serious.'

'What sort of money problems?'

'He owed me a month's rent, by way of example. And he'd bought a very expensive computer on hire-purchase. But as I say—'

'Were you pressing him for payment in any way?' The coroner hesitated. 'I don't mean to suggest that if you had, it would have been at all improper.'

'I didn't press him for payment in any way. He had a good job and he was working very hard and I assumed whatever difficulties he was having were only temporary.'

'So that when you entered the room and discovered the body, it would be fair to say that you were greatly surprised?'

'Surprised and horrified.'

'Horrified. Yes. As would be natural. Thank you, Dr Coyle. I'll now call upon Detective-Inspector Jackson.'

The tall man in rimless glasses had already risen to his feet. Dobie sighed again and did likewise, not to give evidence but to beat an inconspicuous retreat. He'd had about enough. Cantwell was dead and there an end. The rest was tedium. Surprised and horrified. Who wouldn't be?

The crinkly-haired geezer, who as it transpired was in fact the famous Dickie Bird, emerged from the courtroom some forty minutes later and readily accepted Dobie's offer of a lift back to his office. 'Got my own car in for servicing, as it happens. So sitting in on this shindig was a bit damned inconvenient, really. Specially as I didn't have much to say. These your wheels?'

'These are they,' Dobie agreed, opening the door of the Fiesta and clambering in.

'Noticed you in there, of course. In fact I was wondering what you had to do with it.'

'Just an interested observer,' Dobie said. 'At least, I started off that way. I got less interested as time went by.'

'I know just what you mean. Who was that boyo whose name you mentioned?'

'Marryat.'

'I think I remember him. And there used to be a . . . Dr Traynor?'

'He's the head of my department. Mathematics.'

Bird slid a finger inside his shirt collar, the tightness of which appeared to be troubling him. 'Coroner didn't seem to like that bit about the gun. I don't know if you noticed.'

'What bit about the gun?'

'It being unlicensed.'

'Oh? My attention may have wandered at that point. I suppose your wife doesn't ever wear a wig?'

'Eh? . . . I don't have one.'

'I didn't mean *your* wig. A ladies' wig.'

'No, a *wife* is what I don't have. I'm not married. Sorry.'

Dobie continued to drive in silence for the next five

minutes or so, during which time, as he noticed, his passenger appeared to be gripping the handle of the car door with unnecessary tenacity. Bird, breaking the silence, then said, 'Take a right here, if you'd be so good.'

'Pentyrch Road, isn't it?'

'That *is* Pentyrch Road. On the right there.'

'Ah yes. It's a little while since I've been this way.'

The turning having been successfully executed, Bird appeared to relax very slightly. 'Visited us before, have you?'

'Just the once, I think. About five years ago. Of course you've expanded quite a lot since then.'

'Indeed we have. Five years ago? That's before my time, actually. You'll probably hardly recognise the place now. With the new extensions.'

Dobie in fact didn't recognise it, but it wasn't the sort of place you could easily drive past without noticing. Not even Dobie, who was good at that sort of thing. There were considerable expanses of plate glass and laminated concrete, a very large sign that said CORDER ACOUSTICS LTD above a logo design, high iron fencing and a driveway only slightly smaller than that which conducts casual visitors to the front steps of Buckingham Palace. Dobie got the message. 'Here, is it?'

'Nowhere else.'

There was even a security guard at the main gate who, however, waved them through as soon as Bird had wound down the window and advanced his visage through the gap thus provided. Dobie was then directed through an alarming proliferation of white-painted signboards and finally parked the car adjacent to yet another signboard that said ADMIN OFFICES. 'I thought you were in charge of the research section.'

'So I am,' Bird said, dismounting. 'But I can't take you in there, I'm afraid, lot of nonsense no doubt but there it is. We'll go up to my office here and have our little chat. Come along.'

The admin offices, unlike the college buildings, were provided with an efficient lift which whizzed them silently and speedily up to the top floor. Dobie was impressed. 'How many employees do you have working here?'

'You mean in my section? Or overall?'

'All together.'

'Sixty-three on the staff, not counting the cleaners and other odd sods.'

'Good heavens. Five years ago it was Alec Corder and maybe a dozen others.'

'Well, there you are. You *know* Alec then?'

'I used to see more of him than I do now but we haven't altogether lost touch.'

'Yes, that figures. He's pretty busy these days. Okay, come into my parlour.'

Bird's parlour (or cage) had, as Dobie at once acutely observed, all the doings. Plate glass windows, fitted carpet, football-pitch-sized desk and a very youthful secretary whose desk was only very slightly smaller and carried an imposing array of communications equipment. 'Any calls, Wendy?' asked Bird, proceeding as he spoke to his own relatively unimpeded sphere of operations and plumping himself down in the commodious armchair located somewhere in the middle distance behind it.

'Oh yes. Quite a few. On your pad. Hello, Mr Dobie.'

Dobie had heard of secretarial efficiency but this was ridiculous. He turned his head incredulously. 'How did you . . . Oh, it's *Wendy*. I didn't know you worked here.' You couldn't get used to the way these kids sprouted up nowadays. 'Of course it's been some little while . . .'

'Well, I've been here nearly a year now. Dad was keen for me to get to know the ropes sort of thing. So . . .'

'So here you are. How *is* Alec these days?'

'Fine. And Jenny?'

'Yes. I mean, all right. Okay.'

'Wendy, my love,' Bird said, breaking into this cordial exchange of civilities, 'we've had a tedious afternoon and we could use some nice hot coffee. Can do?'

'I think we might manage that,' Wendy said, getting up and heading for the door. Good God, she was as tall as her mother now. Not far short of six feet. But agile with it. Or lissom might be the word. 'So,' Bird said, as the closing door deprived Dobie of this pleasing spectacle, 'you know our little Wendy, then?'

'Not so little now.'

'Indeed she isn't. Take a seat, why don't you? . . . Flits from flower to flower a bit, Wendy does. I don't mind it when she settles in here, but it's a bit of a strain having the boss's daughter typing your letters for you. You always wonder if . . . However. Yes. Cantwell.' Spinning expertly round in his chair, he extracted a green cardboard folder from a filing cabinet. 'Should be all in here. What was it you wanted to know, exactly?'

'I don't quite know what I want to know. That's the trouble. Basically I'm curious as to why he did it.'

'Ah well.' Bird ran his finger cautiously up and down the edge of the folder. 'I don't think I can help you there. Puzzles us all.'

'Would you agree with what that doctor said? That he didn't have any close friends?'

'I wouldn't know what he got up to in his free time, of course. But if you mean here at Corders . . . No, I don't think he did. Most of the people in the section are a good deal older than he was, of course. But he got on with them all right. No friction. I'd know if there was.'

'Why did they put him in R and D in the first place?'

'I expect Alec thought we needed some young blood.' Bird looked up and giggled reflectively. 'Sorry. I should have chosen my words a bit more carefully there. But he was up to the work all right. I'd soon have had him transferred if he wasn't. Ah, here's the coffee.'

In proper cups and saucers, Dobie noted gratefully; no plastic horrors here. Wendy placed these items on the desk and then retired undulatingly to her own demesne, Dobie's appreciative attention, however, being this time focused on the whisky bottle that Bird had produced from some hidden recess under the football pitch. 'A snifter with it?'

'Please,' Dobie said. Offers of this kind he rarely felt able to refuse.

'I reckon we've earned it.'

'The workman is worthy of his hire. What *was* the nature of his work?'

'In broad terms?'

'Yes.'

'Can't give you a detailed answer because we're getting very hot on security these days. But there's nothing very secret about it. What we're doing, we're using laser beams to burn information on to a newly developed kind of magnetic ferrite film, same like in information storage systems. We get the data out again by lower-power laser projection through the film on to a photo-sensing device. Electronic focusing, naturally. Nothing much to it.'

Dobie tried the coffee, which was excellent. The additive material wasn't half bad, either. 'So where do acoustics come into it?'

'Well, the information can relate to sound waves as much as to anything else. And since the laser transmits a light wave, of course, you can make the information damned nearly as detailed as you like. In other words—'

'Compact discs.' Dobie nodded. 'Hi-fi.'

'About the hi-est bloody fi you ever came across. The problem is getting it back into sonics again without using an amplifier the size of this room. That's what Cantwell was working on. And I think I can tell you that between us we reckon we've got it licked.'

'Did *he* think so? I mean, was he enthusiastic?'

'Oh yes. Very. He had to be. Alec's got no use for anyone who's not a hundred and ten per cent behind the job and neither have I.'

Fine. Except it made less sense than ever.

'I saw Wendy this afternoon. My word, she's grown.'

'Wendy?'

'*You* know. Jane's Wendy.'

'Oh.' Jenny turned over a page. 'At the college, was it?'

'No, she's working over at Alec's place.'

'I haven't seen her for quite a while, either. It's a pity, really, they don't get on better.'

'Who, Wendy and Alec?'

'No, no. Wendy and Jane.'

'Don't they?'

'Well, you know Jane. She does tend to be demanding. She'd boss *me* around if I gave her half a chance. Where *is* Alec's place, anyway?'

'Pentyrch Road. It's pretty big now. He must be doing well.'

'What were you doing there?'

'I gave someone a lift back from the inquest.'

'*Inquest?*' This time she actually looked up from her book. '*What* inquest?'

'The one on Sammy Cantwell. I thought I'd go.'

'Whatever for? You're full of surprises.'

'I just felt like it.'

'You *have* been gadding about.' Setting her book down and swinging her legs off the sofa. 'I'm booked to do some travelling myself. The agency rang this morning.'

'Paris again, is it?'

'I have to fly over next Wednesday. For two or three days.'

'Look,' Dobie said. 'You know you don't have to do these jobs if you don't want to.'

'I do want to.'

'That's all right, then.'

'When does *your* vacation start?'

'Next week.'

'I may come back with some ideas. I'll bring the latest brochures.'

'Yes, do that,' Dobie said.

He thought that the earnest-looking lad's efforts had gone to waste but a more detailed search at length revealed a small entry in the morning paper. There was even a modest one-column headline: UNLICENSED GUNS – CORONER HITS OUT. Dobie had observed no such display of pugilistic activity on the coroner's part but was familiar enough with contemporary techniques of reportage to feel no particular surprise, even when he further observed that his ex-student's name had been misspelled in a somewhat embarrassing way. He was now inclined to think that he himself had wasted if not much effort, at any rate a good deal of valuable time the previous day and drove off collegewards in a chastened mood. Leaving Jenny fast asleep, as usual.

But whatever happens, Dobie thought, polluting the mild warmth of the morning with a vast exhalation of tobacco smoke, whatever happens I don't want to become *der zerstreut Professor* of popular legend. Mathematicians have to stay on the ball. Fall back on these nineteenth-century gimmicks and you might as well retire. And I don't want to retire. It's true what Jenny says; I don't have to go on teaching if I don't want to. But I *do* want to.

Not because I'm specially good at it. They don't call me *Drip-Dry* for nothing. There are all kinds of with-it things that other and sprightlier lecturers (such as Wain) might breezily refer to, such as U2 (whatever that was) and Tottenham Hotspur and crack (or was it crash?) and Lenny Henry . . . One could surely bring such things into the study of Wallis's Law, for instance, if only one knew the exact meaning of all those extraordinary concepts. And students such as Hywel Morgan, who frequently multiplied his logarithms, would then surely be on to the exponent of x in a flash. Let the graph of y = 5x represent the parabola described by a regulation football that, having been smartly kicked by Alan Rush (of Morecambe United and Scotland) in the general direction of the goal, is about to be deflected by the opposing scrum-half's forearm . . . No, it was no good. Hopeless. And moreover offside. 'That is why,' Dobie said gloomily, turning away from the long rows of marble and granite plaques, 'a complex number may be represented graphically by a vector, that is to say by trigonometrical notation, which inevitably suggests to our minds the idea of *direction*.' What in actual fact it inevitably suggested to *his* mind was a mental picture of Hywel Morgan writing down the word *direction* and staring at it gloomily. Even that wasn't so bad. But why didn't he have a mental picture of Sammy Cantwell? *That* was bad. *That* was what rankled.

Raising his head and taking another puff at his Super-king, he saw an echoing drift of smoke rise from the chimney of the crematorium, dark smoke sliding away effortlessly downwind.

The sky was otherwise almost free of cloud and the sunlight was etching a gently-moving dapple of tree-leaf shadow around his feet. He had now walked three times the length of the path running from the car park to the cemetery and his shoes, he noticed, had got a little dusty. He turned and looked towards the entrance of the funeral parlour, where a few dark-suited figures were now emerging. Not very many. Only four or five. Dickie Bird was one of them, walking alongside a fatter fair-haired chap; no doubt a colleague. The Corder contingent. Dr Coyle was the last figure to emerge; she stood still for a moment, giving the impression of blinking in the sharp sunlight, then turned away in the opposite direction to the others, walking not towards the car park but down the path upon which Dobie himself was standing. Half-way along it, however, she paused and sat down on a convenient wooden bench. She seemed, as Dobie cautiously approached, to be lost in thought, but looked up sharply enough as he came to a final halt beside her.

'You were at the inquest.'

'Yes,' Dobie said. 'I was.'

'Who are you?'

Her own approach seemed to be pleasingly direct. 'My name's Dobie. John Dobie. May I . . . ?'

'Why not?'

Thus encouraged, Dobie seated himself beside her. 'He was one of my students.'

'Oh. I see.'

'Until last year.'

'I'm afraid I don't remember your name.'

'It's Dobie.'

'My memory's bad but it's not *that* bad. I meant, I don't remember his ever mentioning it.'

'No special reason why he should have done.' At close range, her voice lost its finishing-school tone, seemed huskier and much less self-assured. It sounded better that way. There was even the faintest trace of a Kaird'f accent somewhere underneath. 'He only came to my lectures. That was all.'

'I suppose you're used to speaking to lots of people. You don't get nervous or anything. Me, I'm petrified.'

'So am I, sometimes. Though it's usually all right once you get started. And you did very well, I thought. It wasn't such a very big audience but it's never easy.'

'It was kind of you to come. *My* name's Kate Coyle.'

'I know. Are you really what he said? A police pathologist?'

'I'm a part-time police pathologist. I do night duty and I stand in for Paddy Oates when he's away. Because I need the money. Why do you ask?'

'I just wondered . . . Well, if there was anything . . . ?'

'I didn't do the autopsy. But no, there wasn't anything that would explain it.'

'No medical reason for it?'

'Or any other that I can see.'

She looked different, too, squinting sideways into the bright sunlight. Already it had brought a faint flush to her otherwise rather pallid cheeks. She looked a great deal younger than in the courtroom, more like her true age which Dobie guessed to be somewhere in the middle thirties. Yet still somehow a little worn round the edges. An interesting face, when you looked at it closely.

'I don't think the coroner felt that I did very well. He got quite narky about that bloody gun. Said I should have reported it. The trouble is, he's right. I should have.'

'But otherwise, you're satisfied with the verdict?'

'It seems an odd word to use. But he shot himself all right. Was he a . . . a particularly *bright* student? Or something?'

'He was, yes. And yet,' Dobie said, 'for the last five days I've been trying to remember what he looked like. And I can't.'

'What he *looked* like? . . . Dark-haired. Scruffy. Pathetic.'

'That describes ninety per cent of them. You know, I get to see an awful lot of students, but I hardly ever get to *know* them.'

'Well, I understand that,' Kate said. 'But then why are you . . . ?'

'I don't know. Perhaps I feel a little guilty about it. I feel I *should* be able to remember him.'

'Here.' She opened her handbag. 'See if this helps.'

Dobie took the photograph. It was passport sized and murky in colour, having clearly been taken on one of those do-it-yourself machines, but the facial outlines were clear enough and his recollection was instant. Fidgety Phil. The one whose hands were always moving, playing with a slide-rule, toying with a pencil, riffling a notepad. Front row, right-hand desk. Eyes always moving, too, slithering this way and that. A nervous lad. 'So *that's* Cantwell.'

'Remember him now?'

'Yes.' He gave her back the photograph. 'I'm all right with names, you know. And faces, most of the time. It's putting the two together that I find tricky.'

'It's like that with lots of people.'

'I think,' Dobie said, rather to his own surprise, 'my wife's having an affair.'

Dr Coyle, on the other hand, evinced no surprise at all. 'And I suppose you feel guilty about that, too.'

'Yes, I do. I always thought it would be the other way round. But it isn't.'

'Women don't feel guilty about that sort of thing. Not as a rule.'

'Don't they?'

'We usually rationalise it, somehow. While men tend more to look for some kind of distraction to take their minds off the problem. The usual kind of distraction is another woman. And so it goes on. Ad infinitum.'

'Big fleas and little fleas.'

'Exactly.' Kate studied the distant woods on the hill that lifted itself across the horizon way towards Caerphilly. 'Sammy's a *very* little flea, though, isn't he? Not much of a distraction, really.'

'There's a problem, all the same. A kind of counter-problem.'

'Not a very interesting one. I don't know why he did

it, but if I *did* know it wouldn't bring him back. Nothing can do that.'

She had lowered her head again and appeared to be studying the shape of her hands, which again lay folded upon her dark-skirted lap. Small pale hands with neat blunt fingernails. *She* was anything but fidgety. And yet, Dobie thought, that outward relaxation, here as in the courtroom, somehow conveyed the sense of some deeper inward tension. He said, 'Do people often talk to you like this?'

'Of course they talk to me. I'm a doctor.'

'That's not what I meant.'

Kate, who knew that it wasn't, nodded and said, 'Yes, they do. All the time.'

'People used to talk to *me* a lot. I got very tired of it, of listening to problems and so forth. So in the end I sort of shut myself off. It isn't hard to do. In fact it's easy.'

'I know.'

'But don't *you* do that,' Dobie said.

He saw that she was crying. Female tears invariably embarrassed him, but not on this occasion; it was obvious that she had something to cry *about* and that these indeed were not female tears but the true *lacrimae rerum*, a celebration of that great star-laden sadness that sometimes moved behind mathematical symbols as he manoeuvred them across the emptiness of a paper page. Of course he got tired of it. Anyone would. But it was a celebration for all that. He felt in his pocket and discovered there a large white cotton handkerchief, which Kate accepted.

'Can we maybe talk more later? About Sammy?'

'It won't help,' Kate said indistinctly.

'Not him, no. But it might help *me*.'

He got up and walked away down the dusty path. Kate, inaudibly sniffling, watched him go. After a while she put the handkerchief, not very noticeably dampened, into her handbag. She felt a little better now, she thought.

More relaxed.

The telephone was ringing as Dobie entered his flat. Nobody, as was evident, was there to answer it. Only us chickens. He bolted into the sitting-room and grabbed the receiver.

'Yes? . . . Yes . . . Oh hullo, Jane.'

No hurry after all. He pulled up a chair and sat down on it, panting slightly. 'Look, I've just this moment got back myself, I don't think she's in.'

'You I'd like to speak to.'

'What?'

'I *said*, it's *you* I wanted to speak to.' Jane had the habit, when speaking to him over the telephone, of enunciating with exceptional clarity and in tones one might normally use when addressing foreigners, total imbeciles or golden retrievers. And not only over the telephone, either. This always made Dobie feel and even speak (when an occasion arose) like Bertie Wooster. 'Oh, right-ho,' he said.

'Are you there?' the voice said suspiciously. Are you *all* there, was what its tone implied.

'I think so. I mean yes, I am. Definitely. Cogito ergo sum.'

'I'm glad to find you in such high spirits. In fact I'm glad to find you at all. I've been trying to get through to you most of the day. I want to have a little *chat* with you, John. Privately.'

'Oh, right. Fire away.'

'No, not over the telephone *if* you don't mind.' No one but a congenital idiot would have conceived of such a plan, as was now obvious. 'Are you free tomorrow evening?'

'Well, I'm rather bogged down this week,' Dobie said. 'Exam papers and such. And Jenny's off to Paris day after tomorrow, did she tell you? . . . Oh. She did.

What about Friday? I finish work on Friday. What about Friday evening, say around—'

'Let's say at exactly eight o'clock.'

'Fine.' Dobie took out his pocket diary and scribbled in it furiously.

'Now you won't just *forget* about it, John? I know when you're busy you often tend—'

'No, no, I've written it down, look forward to it.'

'Bye then.' The phone clicked in his ear. Dobie, perceiving that in his haste he had made the appropriate entry for eight a.m. on the Thursday morning, drew a little arrow to rectify the error and put his diary away in his coat pocket.

It was odd about Jane. Certainly there was nothing remotely Aunt Agatha-like in her appearance, which was that of a tall well-manicured fluffy blonde well preserved for her age which had to be about the same as Dobie's. Which was forty-eight. All the same, Jenny was right. She was bossy. An eye like Ma's, as Bertie would have put it, to threaten and command. And since she was, in point of concrete fact, Wendy's Ma, no doubt Wendy felt the same way about it. In view of this general agreement, then, it was odd that Jenny should have taken to her quite so strongly. Perhaps Jane supplied a certain element that was lacking in her married life. Dobie wasn't bossy. Certainly not.

Ineffectual, more like it. Maybe *that* was why she'd got the blonde wig. In imitation, conscious or otherwise, of Jane. Well, you had to admit Jane's turn-out was always impeccable. As befitted a very rich man's consort. If it was elegance you were after, Jenny couldn't really compete. Which mightn't stop her from trying, all the same.

Nothing you can do to help, Kate Coyle had said. But that hadn't stopped him from trying, either. Ineffectually, of course. At the police station, where he'd stopped on the way back home, the fuzz had barely given him the time of day. What had been the big copper's name? I'm all right with names, Dobie thought. Most of the time. Superintendent . . .

Pontin.

That was it.

'. . . I'm not *questioning* the cause of death,' Dobie had said plaintively. 'What I want to know is why he did it.'

'Why he did what?'

'Killed himself.'

'Oh, he'll have had his reasons,' Pontin said.

'Yes, but what *are* they? Nobody seems to have come up with anything. And it seems there wasn't any letter or anything like that. Suicides usually leave letters, don't they? – or *some* kind of indication why they—'

'Offhand, sir, I can't give you the exact statistics, but I'm pretty sure some bloke or other will have worked them out by now. Fed 'em into a computer, like as not. That's what happens to everything these days, far as I can see. I don't believe too much in all that stuff meself. It's still the old-fashioned bobby on the beat who brings the villains in, don't you be in any two minds on *that* score, Mr Robey. They may have all them machines an' stuff up at the Yard—'

'Then why do *you* think he did it?'

'Now look, sir, I'm just a policeman. A public servant. I can't afford to spend much of my time in *thinking*. In fact that's part of the trouble, if you ask me. These kids who go to the colleges, they're highly strung. Intellectual, you know what I mean? Could be he didn't have any reason at all that you or I would recognise. Just sits there thinking to himself and then he ups and does it. It's all got to do with the strain of modern life.'

'You could have something there,' Dobie said.

Looking down at the notepad upon which he had been doodling, he saw that he had covered the page with squiggly representations of the Eiffel Tower. Curious, that.

There was a strong wind blowing at the airport and Dobie stood on the waving base with his shoulders hunched and his hands driven deep into his pockets, watching Jenny walk briskly with the other passengers towards the waiting 727. When she turned to look back he waved, since that's what waving bases are for, and she raised the hand that wasn't carrying her holdall and then walked on. Back on Saturday. That's if I don't get held up.

The plane took off on time, anyway.

Driving back, Dobie slipped one of his favourite tapes into the cassette-player. The C major string quintet, K.515. But not even the lilt of the opening theme did much to soothe his sense of unease. At the roundabout he turned left, heading not back home but for Culverhouse Cross and Cardiff. He didn't want to go back to the flat. Not just yet.

He stopped some way short of the castle and got out the street map. Ludlow Road was off the City Road and appeared to be a cul-de-sac. There was, as he soon discovered, nothing very prepossessing about it; the usual drab late-Victorian houses ran to either side of it, alleviated here and there by glass shop frontages. About halfway down on the left-hand side, however, someone had plonked down a modern supermarket of modest size, its windows filled with posters announcing various cut-price offers and bearing the pine-tree logo of a well-known supermarket chain. Dobie, parking opposite, wondered if there was anything he wanted to buy but couldn't think of anything; Jenny would certainly have left the pantry shelves and the fridge well stocked. Number 12, almost directly opposite, was a solidly-built (as Kate had said) two-storey construction conforming pretty much to the general and depressing pattern of the other houses in the street; it bore, however, an inscribed plaque which said:

DR CAITLIN COYLE
Consulting Hours
1000 - 1230
1700 - 1900

Three worn stone steps led up to the front door. Dobie climbed them.

Cantwell's rooms were decidedly a cut above the usual student digs. Luxurious, no. But spacious and comfortable. Two armchairs, adequately cushioned, had been placed to either side of a three-bar electric fire with two small tables conveniently adjacent; the bed, on the far side of the room, was plumply mattressed and an electric radio-cum-alarm-clock stood on the night table, its large digital figures greenly glowing. Nearby was an enormous wardrobe, Edwardian in its majesty, and an almost equally capacious chest of drawers. Along the far wall were shelves that held a couple of dozen textbooks, a rather swish Sony cassette-player and a few cassette boxes, while right-angled to it was a work-desk, much less impressively dimensioned than the monstrosity in Dickie Bird's office but sizeable, none the less, offering adequate space for an IBM computer and monitor, a Smith Corona word processor and several loose-leaf notebooks. 'Is all this stuff valuable?' Kate asked. 'It looks as though it might be.'

'I wouldn't throw any of it away. IBM computers aren't cheap.'

'I don't know what to do with it.'

'Pack it up,' Dobie suggested, 'until the next of kin claims it. There was an uncle or something, wasn't there? I don't know what the legal position is otherwise. Did he leave a will?'

'I don't think so. Anyway I've no idea how you . . . disassemble the thing.'

'I can do that for you, if you like. I'll find some boxes. Of course you don't know the guy's address.'

'The uncle? No. I doubt if he's even been notified.'

'Didn't he have an address book?' Dobie had opened one of the notebooks and was glancing through it.

'If he did, nobody's found it.'

'He may have got it on database.'

'On what?'

'On the computer. Did the police check on it? Probably not, if the one I spoke to's anything to go by. He didn't hold with computers and all that modern rubbish.'

'Who was that?'

'Superintendent Pontin.'

'Oh, Pontin, yes. He's a right berk. Crowd control at football matches, that's what he likes best. Reckons he could improve on Hillsborough if they gave him a chance and I bet he bloody well would.'

'He certainly wasn't very informative,' Dobie admitted. He swivelled the desk chair around and seated himself at the computer. 'We may get more cooperation out of this. Let's see.'

Kate watched him as his fingers first stroked, then tapped the keyboard, his gaze focused the while on the monitor screen. 'You're one of those clever buggers, are you?'

'You don't have to be very clever. Just persistent.'

'Professor of Mathematics and all.'

The fingers didn't pause. 'Yes. But *I* didn't tell you that.'

'I checked you out,' Kate said.

She saw that an elliptical figure had appeared on the monitor screen. Another then walked across to superimpose itself on the first. Then another. The fingers stopped tapping. Instead they reached across for the notebook, flipped through its pages. Paused again.

'Ah,' Dobie said.

Tap. Tap. Tap. The figure on the screen began to spin round on itself, fluctuating wildly. Kate's head had now moved close to Dobie's as they stared at it together. '*That's* what he was doing,' Dobie said.

'What?'

'He was looking for a strange attractor.'

'A *what*?'

'There it is. See?'

'All I can see is a circle thing spinning round.'

Dobie tapped another key and the shape disappeared. Just like that.

'No addresses. No database. Just some work he brought home.'

'Oh well. You tried.'

Dobie was turning the pages of the notebook again. 'He was using a fairly simple Lorenz equation. But some of the others here are a bit more complex. Anyway, it all has to do with what's called the butterfly effect.'

'And what's that?'

'It's the effect on global climate which is brought about by a single beat of a butterfly's wings. It's sort of a hypothetical . . . Ah. I can see you think I'm joking.'

'Mathematicians don't joke, do they?'

'Don't they just?' Dobie leaned back in his chair, a little tiredly. 'The whole of advanced mathematics these days is just one huge practical joke. Because that's what the universe appears to be. Beyond a certain point there's no rhyme or reason to it. So what you do is, you try to locate that point. The point at which the scientifically predictable ceases to be so. In wave mechanics, things like that.'

'You mean the butterfly is the fly in the ointment.'

'In so far as you'd *like* things to be predictable, yes.

And physicists certainly do. But mathematics isn't like that. If everything's predictable, life's bound to get a bit damned dull. And mathematics *can't* be dull, by definition. There's always got to be something to find out or there's no point in doing it at all.'

'Funny,' Kate said. 'Most people think just the opposite.'

'That's because they know it can't happen. Maybe for a while things can go round and round in a nice smooth orbit, like you saw on the screen there. But then some unknown factor, like the butterfly, interferes and attracts the particles – pulls them out of the pattern. And it all goes haywire. We call that factor a strange attractor. It's *strange* in the sense of *alien*, something that can't be included in the original equation. It's quite a frivolous little object otherwise.'

'Is that how you spend your time? Chasing frivolous little objects?'

'For months on end,' Dobie said. 'They're elusive. They take a lot of catching. And when you've caught one, as like as not you don't know what to do with it. I suspect that's what happened to Sammy. In the end he left it where it was. Trapped inside the computer.'

'Poor little thing,' Kate said. 'I know how it feels.'

'Yes,' Dobie said. 'So do I.'

He got up and went to sit down in one of the armchairs instead. Yes. Very comfy. It wasn't a bad little room at all. He liked it here.

'. . . I've just seen my wife off at the airport. She's gone to Paris.'

Kate sat down opposite him, not properly but perching herself on the upholstered arm. 'Gone for long?'

'No,' Dobie said. 'Not for long.'

'Is that another dismantling job you have to do?'

'I don't know,' Dobie said.

'Better dismantled than broken into pieces, don't you think?'

'That seems logical, Captain. But then we're not all Mister Spocks. People *aren't* logical.'

'Women even less so than men?'

'I didn't say that.'

'More subject to their emotions, perhaps?'

'Perhaps. Or to strange attractors.'

'How long have you been married, anyway?'

'Not quite a year.'

'Oh well, shit, you have to give it a bit more of a chance than *that.*'

'That's what *I* can't help feeling,' Dobie admitted.

The noise of an aircraft, passing high overhead, came to them both as a distant whisper.

Friday morning. End of term. Everybody frantically trying to finish marking exam papers, except for Dobie. He'd finished his already. But there was a packet of stuff just arrived from George Campbell at MIT, six mini-discs loaded with computations, and to judge from George's accompanying letter some of the new sets were exciting. 'That should keep you busy through the summer,' Mary Mayfield said. Mary Mayfield was the departmental secretary. She was very nice.

'What about your own plans? Spain again this year?'

'Yes, I got an early booking. I'm off Monday. Six nice long weeks on the Costa del Concrete, should be fun.'

'I'm sure it will be,' Dobie said. 'I expect my wife's got something up her sleeve for me. But I don't know what it is.'

'She's in the business, isn't she? So she ought to . . . Oh, by the way. Telephone call for you. Earlier this morning.'

'What, from Jenny?'

'No. A Mrs Corder.' Mary was checking the indecipherable scrawl on her notepad. 'Eight o'clock tonight, was that right?'

'Yes, you needn't have bothered. I hadn't forgotten.'

'Well, she says can you make it at her place instead of yours?'

The Corders' house was the far side of Porthkerry Park, twenty miles distant at least with some nasty bumpy stretches. Dobie sighed. 'I suppose so.'

'That's good because I said you could.'

At five o'clock, to make matters worse, it started to rain and by half-past seven it was pelting. Doubtless, Dobie thought as he peered astigmatically through the blurred windscreen, Jane that morning had had a peremptory word with a passing butterfly and her resultant accurate assessment of the forthcoming global climate had decided her to conduct such interviews as she had arranged for that evening cosily at home. It was, after all, a very palatial home. Dobie had only visited it two or three times before, but he had been impressed. You were *meant* to be impressed. It was placed on a narrow promontory thrusting out across the Bristol Channel, so close to the sea that in rough weather the waves sloshed right across the portholes, and its trendy-architect bungalow design included all manner of refinements and creature comforts, which (or so Dobie hoped) might well include a little something to warm the cockles, after a drive like this one. The house was called Pantmawr. Nobody knew why. Though of course you had to call it something.

There was a large gravelled space outside where Dobie halted his steed, punctiliously leaving a clear space through to the front gate from the double garage in the corner (which anyway was closed). He checked the time before getting out. Three minutes to eight. Very punctual. The rain was still fairly whizzing down and he felt in no great hurry to leave his agreeably bottom-warmed car seat. To the south the horizon was dark with scudding clouds, black as a kookaburra's khyber and obscuring what on a less inhospitable evening would have been a spectacular sunset. He could just make out a few vague lights twinkling half-heartedly on the Somerset coast. The prospect of a little something continued to beckon him and he got out of the car and squelched purposefully over to the front door, loose gravel crunching under his feet.

Tie straight? Flies zipped up?

Yes.

About to press the doorbell, he saw that a sheet of paper had been folded and tucked neatly under the brass knocker that provided an alternative, if unseemly, method of announcing one's arrival. He took it and unfolded it. It said:

BACK SOON PLEASE GO IN MAKE YOURSELF AT HOME

This message had been typed in red, for some unfathomable reason, and Jane's squiggly signature appended in purple ink. Dobie tried the door. It was open all right. And of course all this was typical. He went through into the hallway, left his raincoat on a convenient hook and walked on into the sitting-room, which seemed to be rather more than comfortably warm. Central heating on, in midsummer. Probably no one had bothered to turn it off.

He glanced at the note again before dropping it on to one of the side tables. He wondered what SOON meant. Probably anything from five to forty-five minutes. At least it was clear what MAKE YOURSELF AT HOME meant, and he saw that a whisky decanter and tumbler had been placed on a table beside the cocktail bar, in a shaded alcove on the far side of the room. Jane was an irritating woman, but she had her points. It was five past eight now and the sun well over the yardarm, time for a stengah, what? . . . Dobie giggled foolishly to himself as he listened to the pleasant trickle of Glenlivet Double Malt tilting into the waiting tumbler; there *was* something a bit memsahib-ish about old Jane, with her ruthless concern for the welfare of the natives and other lesser breeds without the law, such as men in general. Give 'em whisky and make 'em wait; in university circles she'd end up a Vice-Chancellor, nothing was more certain. Whereas Jenny . . .

Dobie took a healthy swig at the contents of his glass (no sensible man would pollute Glenlivet with water, much less soda) and turned away. He'd no idea where Jenny would end up. At the present rate of striking she'd be lucky if this time next year she wasn't being shipped off to South America or Mauritania or some such awful place, and when she got there she wouldn't even enjoy it. He gazed glumly at the array of photographs on the mantelpiece. Jane was there all right, both in a posed studio shot and (looking naturally very much younger) in a wedding photograph, clutching the right arm of a correspondingly youthful Alec. Another black-and-white shot of an even younger Jane clad in an abbreviated swimsuit and bathing cap turned out, on closer examination, to be a photograph of Wendy; there seemed to be some kind of cup or sporting trophy on a small table somewhere in the background, but either the camera was slightly out of focus or else (and more probably) Dobie was. Further along the mantelpiece Alec was genially keeping up the good work, shaking hands with the Prince of Wales; this one had an inscription that said 'Prince of Wales' Industrial Award – Corder Acoustics, Cardiff'. The award itself, which appeared to be a small silver plaque, was mounted on a wooden shield directly alongside. There was writing on the plaque also, but Dobie couldn't read it. Odd, that. The light was decidedly dim here, but even so.

And still no sign of Jane. Dobie went back to the alcove and sat down on the leather-backed couch behind the table. He took off his glasses, polished them with his handkerchief and put them back on. Everything still seemed to be fogged at the edges. He listened to the drumming patter of raindrops on the roof.

'Not here,' he heard himself say in quite a loud voice. 'Gone to Parish.' He giggled again, this time audibly and took another shwig of whishky, why the hell not, Alec had crates of the shtuff down in the sheller. Then he took off his glasses again and rubbed his eyes. Then sat back on the couch and closed them. A warm glow of well-being radiated outwards from his stomach. The steady beat of the raindrops was soporific. Shopo — Yes. Soporific. He felt woozhy but pleasantly woozhy. Piles of cotton-wool-like clouds drifted peacefully across the horizon.

Dobie slept.

He woke up very abruptly and at once decided that he wasn't feeling all that great. Something was wrong and he didn't know what. He could still hear the rhythmic beat of raindrops but over and above that sound there was a very loud screaming whine that it took him a moment or two to identify as the sound of a jet engine, of an aircraft passing very low overhead. It was that sound, he realised, that had woken him up.

For the rest he knew exactly where he was and what he was doing; he was sitting on a couch in Jane Corder's house and he had just drunk a glass of whisky and had dropped off to sleep but that had to be wrong because his face felt stiff and everything looked wonky . . . Perhaps I'm ill, he thought, and they've put me to bed. Why didn't I wake up before? Good God, perhaps I *did* pass out, how else could they have . . . ? How very silly/odd/embarrassing/frightening. Frightening because I can't move my arms or my legs and that's because I've been TIED UP . . . HELP HELP! But this is just bloody ridiculous, incredible . . .

All of that but none the less true. His wrists had been tied, not painfully but securely, behind his back and his ankles similarly fastened, not with a rope but with what looked like somebody's tie. Peering downwards with difficulty, Dobie recognised the tie as his own. Such pain as he felt – which was really more of a marked discomfort – came from the region of his mouth, which someone had thoughtlessly sealed up with what had to be a wide strip of sticking plaster. He had already made, inadvertently, a rather disgusting gugging noise; he didn't attempt to make any further sounds, but listened instead. Apart from the thump of the falling rain and the fast-receding thrum of the aircraft engine, he couldn't hear anything. All was silent.

His vision still seemed to be slightly hazy but he remembered now he'd taken his glasses off and put them on the table. There they were, beside the whisky decanter and the almost-empty tumbler. But even without them he could see quite clearly the face of the ornamental clock on the far wall, the hands of which now showed twenty to nine. Twenty to *nine*? He'd been sleeping, then, for something like half an hour. Unless it was twenty to nine in the morning but no, that wasn't possible, the electric light was still burning in the corner and the curtains still drawn and there was an armchair over there with its back towards him and someone was sitting in it.

Burglars, of course. He'd been tied up by a burglar. That seemed to be the only rational explanation. But what would a burglar be doing sitting in an armchair?

Nothing very much. Just sitting there. Dobie could make out the shape of an elbow protruding over the side-arm of the chair, and above the chair the outline of a rather weird pork-pie-type hat. The elbow was clad in grey cloth, in all probability part of a grey raincoat; not of a jacket or suit, anyway. So whoever it was, it certainly wasn't Jane. Dobie's first and somewhat hysterical reaction, in fact, was to imagine that he had somehow become converted into a disembodied spirit and that the fellow sitting in the armchair was he himself, or anyway his own doppelganger. This quirk of fancy, obviously unworthy of a university mathematician, could only be excused by the weird situation in which the said mathematician now found himself . . . Not, mind you, that Lewis Carroll hadn't been on to something with all that business of mirror-images, a great deal of work remained to be done in the matter of resolving left-right transferences into the appropriate polar equations; but (Dobie decided) this probably wasn't the best time to do it. Getting himself ungagged and unbound was an evident number one priority; since, however, the bloke in the armchair was almost certainly the person who had thus rendered him helpless, there couldn't be very much point in making gug-gugging noises at him. Which took you back to square one. Burglars don't sit down in armchairs, do they? – when they're on the job; they get on with burgling as a sensible person should. It was all very mysterious and inexplicable.

And uncomfortable, of course. Though really he'd had little time in which to register the degree of his discomfort; the whisper of the descending aircraft was still just audible although the power of the jets had now been cut – clearly it was coming in to land at Rhoose airport. And now, however, things appeared to be happening back here at the ranch. The burglar, rising abruptly from the chair to afford Dobie a brief glimpse of a grey belted raincoat with a turn-up collar (similar to those affected at one time in his distinguished career by the late Humphrey Bogart), had begun to behave in an altogether more burglar-like way, padding swiftly but silently across the beige carpet and finally disappearing altogether from Dobie's angle of vision, this to the sound of a gently closed door. The kitchen door, if Dobie's recollections of the house's geography were correct. He commenced at once to wriggle about, like a worm on a hook. He couldn't either unfasten or break the knots at his wrists but he might, he thought, be able, once the coast was clear, to retrace the steps of the burglar in a series of wallaby-like hops and, once in the kitchen, discover some more effective way of freeing himself from his bonds. A nice sharp knife, for example. While savouring in advance the beauty of this ingenious plan, he heard the front door come open and then close. The burglar had gone.

Thank heaven for *that*.

Leaning forward and about to initiate the first of his kangaroo-jumps, he heard sharp, firm footsteps coming from the hallway and realised that he had misinterpreted the situation. It wasn't that the burglar had left. Somebody else had come in. They sounded to him like female footsteps. A moment later, this impression was confirmed as he heard Jane's voice, calling him in puzzled and somewhat disgruntled tones. 'Dobie? . . . John? Where *are* you?'

She ought, of course, to be apprised of the situation that had arisen. 'Mmmmm-mmmmmm,' Dobie said.

He didn't think she'd heard him, and it soon became obvious that she hadn't. She stood for a moment or two by the sitting-room door, gazing this way and that; she was wearing a raincoat, too, a very *wet* raincoat, which no doubt accounted in part for her disgruntlement. Having failed to locate him in the dimness of the alcove where he crouched, she looked, still in some perplexity, towards the kitchen door and then advanced towards it. 'Oh my God, John . . . What are you up to *now*?'

'Mum-mum-mum-mum,' Dobie remarked.

A moment after she had vanished from view he heard the side door open again and the footsteps pause, then an unpleasant thumping sort of noise, as though the door, in opening, had run into some kind of hard and fixed obstruction. A gasp. A slithery sound. A thud. Then silence.

The aircraft had to have landed by now.

Oh *Jesus*, Dobie thought.

The sounds that he had just heard could be given an alternative explanation. A nastier one. It was at least feasible that someone had hit Jane very forcibly on the head. This wild theory gained in feasibility as the silence continued. Other hypotheses might no doubt be put forward, but right now Dobie couldn't think of any. He was feeling much too scared. Too scared to think straight. Much too scared, in fact, to think at all. He listened, instead.

Now there were other sounds. Sounds as of a heavy weight being pulled or dragged across the kitchen floor. Other soft sounds, impossible to decipher. Then a sharp click and a rattle, the sort of noise made by a sliding doorbolt, a bolt that hadn't been very recently oiled. Then silence again. Though the sound of the falling rain, that had been going on for so long now as to seem a part of the silence, seemed to have become a little louder. And a steady current of cold air seemed to be entering the room from somewhere. After a while, and emanating as it seemed from outside the house, the sound of what had to have been a pretty loud splash. Dobie felt suddenly very cold. He shivered.

Hopping was easier than he'd thought it would be. And a beneficial form of exercise, really. The great thing was not to lose his balance and fall over, since he had the feeling that if he did that, he wouldn't be able to get up again.

He didn't fall down. The kitchen door had been left open and the light was switched on, so he could see at once that the kitchen was empty. So far, so good. He was scared all right, but not quite as scared as he'd been before. The next few minutes, though, were extremely frustrating. He had to fumble open sideboard drawers with his fingertips and then turn himself awkwardly around to peer into their dark interiors. When at long last he found where the kitchen knives were kept, it was only to discover that holding the knife by the handle he couldn't angle the blade sufficiently to saw at his bonds, though he did manage to inflict a nasty cut on his middle finger in the process. Thinking then and belatedly of an ingenious ruse which a more assiduous watcher of TV serials would have hit upon at once, he contrived cunningly to wedge the knife, sharp edge downwards, in the crack of a closed drawer and through this means eventually to reduce half of an expensive blue silk tie (his own) to ribbons. Dealing with the other half then presented, of course, no kind of a problem. Unhobbled but breathing deeply, Dobie walked over to the back door, which stood ajar, opened it fully and peered cautiously out.

He knew what was out there, in a general sense. A twelve-foot-wide tiled balcony used, in the summer months, as a sunbathing patio but now awash with rain. There were white plastic reclining chairs, getting wet, and a small white plastic table where, under more congenial conditions, tall glasses of cooling refreshments might be placed. At the far end there was a wrought-iron parapet, about three feet high, and beyond the parapet there was a sheer drop of some twelve feet to the open sea, now snarling and gurgling in a thoroughly inhospitable way. On a clear day you could see right across the Channel to the Watchet hills. Tonight you couldn't. Looking in the other direction on even a miserable day you could see the roof of the double garage and the steps that led down from the patio towards it. Tonight you couldn't. Tonight it was dark as pitch and the rain was still coming down in sheets. Dobie went back inside.

In the sitting-room he picked up the telephone and dialled 999. 'Get me the police,' he said crisply. 'This is an emergency.' That, at least, was what he *meant* to say. What he actually said was, 'Mmmmmm-mmmm-mmmm.' He'd forgotten about the bloody sticking-plaster. He reached up and ripped it off, over-hurriedly. 'Owwwwwwwwww,' he said, in a high shrill excited voice.

The telephone operator seemed unimpressed. 'What service did you require, madam?'

'I'm not a madam, I'm me, I mean it's a man. I want the police.'

'*One* moment, madam,' the operator said.

2

'Very inclement weather tonight,' Inspector Jackson observed.

'It is indeed.'

'For being called out, I mean, on *this* kind of a caper.'

Jackson was, like most policemen, a patient man and one, moreover, well accustomed to dealing with amiable (and some not so amiable) lunatics. He had, indeed, only that morning been summoned forth to investigate the case of one Henrietta Byrd, reported missing, possibly kidnapped, from her parents' home; Henrietta had turned out to be a budgerigar, this somewhat to Jackson's chagrin. The facts of the Henrietta Byrd affair, however, he had elucidated pretty quickly – as soon, indeed, as the bereaved owner had shown him Henrietta's cage, forlornly empty; while the facts that this Dobie character was recounting seemed to make very little sense at all. 'What it all boils down to, sir, is that you feel you've reason to suspect a crime to have been committed, but you're far from being sure as to its actual *nature*. Does that sum it up fairly?'

'Except that she's gone. Jane has. Mrs Corder.'

'Ah, but gone *where*, if you see what I mean? I take it there's a Mr Corder about?'

'Oh yes.'

'So where's he?'

'I've no idea,' Dobie said. 'He may be still at his office. Corder Acoustics. In Cardiff.'

Jackson looked at his wrist-watch. 'A bit late for that, isn't it?'

'He does work late most days.'

'But he *lives* here, I suppose? . . . Well, I expect we can trace him without too much trouble. But maybe we shouldn't notify him until things are a little clearer. Let's see now. Last seen wearing. The lady had on a raincoat, I think you said?'

'Navy blue raincoat, yes. The sort with the hood thing you can pull up over your head. I couldn't see much else but she was wearing dark slacks, I think they were navy blue as well. And shoes, of course. Black shoes.'

'Not boots?'

'No, definitely not boots. Shoes. With flat heels.'

Sober, Jackson had already decided. And even coherent. Up to a point. Going by what Dobie *said*, there had to be at the very least a strong presumption of foul play, but the presumption didn't seem to be strong enough to justify the pressing of all the alarm bells. Jackson flipped his notebook shut. 'I'll ask you to excuse me for just a moment, sir . . .'

Detective-Sergeant Box was in the kitchen, gazing gloomily at the floor. Red and ochre tiles, not very revealing. There were marks on it all right, but then there are marks on most kitchen floors. 'Find anything?'

'Bit of blood,' Box said, with no very marked relish. 'Over by the sink.'

'Says he cut himself trying to get loose.'

'Yes, there's blood on the knife blade too. No more'n a drop. Wasn't a stabbing, whatever else may have happened.'

'Puzzle, isn't it,' Jackson said. It wasn't a question. He picked up one of the frayed strips of silk that Box had collected and carefully placed on the kitchen table, surveyed it, put it down again. 'Check the car?'

'Yes. In the garage. Motor's warm. The Fiesta, that's Mr Dobie's. Checked that, too.'

'Warm?'

'No. Cooled off. Been out in the rain.'

Jackson fingered his lip thoughtfully. When all was said and done . . . two cars here and only one person. 'We'll have that knife anyway. *And* the whisky decanter. When the hell's that Evans going to get here?'

'Probably lost his way.'

'Wouldn't surprise me.'

There wasn't much more that he could do until the dabs sergeant arrived. Nothing he could reasonably hold Dobie for, either. No body. No blood. No signs of struggle. Nothing. He clumped sadly back to the sitting-room.

'Perhaps you won't mind coming round to the station in the morning, sir, to make a formal statement. By then perhaps we'll have got things cleared up here a little. You say you're a professor at the university?'

'Yes,' Dobie said. This was one of the few things he felt relatively sure about.

'Wonder if that's what's behind all this business of tying you up? Them students get up to all manner of larks. You wouldn't believe.'

'You mean you think all this is some kind of practical joke?'

'I'm not saying it *is*, mind. But it could be. Perverted sense of humour is what they got, some of them.' Jackson shook his head sadly. 'Or here's another line of thought. That whisky you drank, now . . .'

'Yes, I'd thought of that. Perhaps it was drugged. That could be why I—'

'Well, we'll be checking on that. Nothing easier. And *if* it was and we can see what kind of drug it is we're dealing with . . .'

'You're thinking in terms of one that might induce hallucinations?'

'I'm thinking out loud is what I'm doing. But these kids get their hands on some very funny stuff these days, there's no denying it. I've come across some cases—'

'*What* kids?' Dobie then began to speak very rapidly. 'Unless it was that chap in the raincoat, he could have got here ahead of me and been in the house all the time – *I* wouldn't have known, see what I mean? The front door wasn't locked so suppose he got here before I did, read that note, went on in—'

He certainly seems, Jackson thought, to have had a nasty shock. No doubt about that. And that car in the garage wasn't a hallucination, either. Though, of course . . . 'About that note, sir. What did it say, exactly?'

'The point is it wasn't addressed specifically to me. Someone else might have read it and thought . . .' Dobie's head was aching rather badly now. He closed his eyes for a moment. 'It's over there on that table. You can read it for yourself.'

'No, it isn't.'

Dobie opened his eyes again. 'It isn't?'

'No, sir. That's where you *said* you put it but it isn't there now. Hence my question.'

'It said, "Back soon" – I remember wondering how soon "soon" would be – and then "Go in and make yourself at home," or something like that. It was typed in red ink and the paper had got a bit damp so the ink was a bit smeary. But not so you couldn't read it.'

'She was *expecting* you, you said – at eight o'clock?'

'And I got here exactly on time.'

'Then why wasn't *she* here?'

'I don't know. The note didn't say.'

Jackson had made a note, too, in his little black notebook. He read through it again.

Poss. burglar (?)
tall medium build
grey belted raincoat + funny hat
heard dragging noise + splash

'An odd business, then,' he said, 'and no mistake.'

Dobie sat down heavily in the armchair. His own armchair in his own sitting-room. Home sweet home. Looking round him, he didn't think much of it. But then right now he was trying not to think too much about *anything*.

After a while he got up and started to prowl round in slow pantherine circles. He was afraid of dropping off to sleep again and being thus perhaps caught up in some endless Yeatsian cycle . . . Silly, but there it was. What kind of a drug would knock you out like that, anyway? A Mickey something? Maybe in the morning he'd give a ring to Peter Draycott or any other of the Pharmacology boys who might happen to be still around. On the first day of the summer vacations. What a way to start them.

In the morning, though. Not now. Though in fact it wasn't really all that late. Just gone ten. Incredible. He hadn't yet had anything to eat, but his head was paining him and he wasn't hungry.

What he chiefly needed, he thought, was a cup of black coffee and some aspirin, followed by a restful hour with the Heutling String Quartet. He wended his way, therefore, to the bedroom to get the aspirin bottle, which would, he thought, be reposing in the drawer of Jenny's night table, where she usually kept it. Switching on the overhead light, he observed with no great sense of surprise that Jane Corder was lying stretched out on top of the bed without very much in the way of clothes on. She appeared to be dead. He felt no great surprise because, naturally, he didn't believe it. He advanced, nevertheless, upon the bed in order to . . . you know . . . investigate.

His investigation revealed that Jane Corder was lying stretched out on top of the bed without very much in the way of clothes on. She appeared to be dead. She *was* dead. 'Oh my God,' Dobie said. 'Oh my God. Oh my God. Whatever next.' Jane Corder didn't reply, but he wasn't really talking to *her*, anyway.

The pain in his head had suddenly become murderous, as though his brains were leaking slowly out through the back of his skull. It couldn't be Jane. Clearly it couldn't. But it was. He couldn't see her clothes anywhere, apart from the (normally) fetching black bra-and-pantie set that was all she was wearing. A large bath towel, however, was lying on the floor at his feet; he picked it up and drew it carefully over the corpse, shrouding her decently from head to feet. He knew that he shouldn't really have touched anything, but knew also that he couldn't let her go on lying there like *that*. It wasn't nice.

He turned and made a bolt for the French window, which fortunately wasn't locked; he had time, therefore, to get out on to the balcony before being sick. Vomiting had at least the side-effect of seeming, if only temporarily, to ease his headache. When he had finished throwing up he went back to the sitting-room, picked up the telephone and dialled Jane's number. He thought that with any luck the police would still be there.

They were.

Jackson, Box and the hitherto elusive Sergeant Evans were there within twenty minutes. Half an hour later, Detective-Superintendent Pontin arrived. Not, it must be said, in the best of tempers.

'What we got here then, Jackson?'

'What you might call complications, sir,' Jackson said.

'Just what we don't need. Now I don't want any nonsense with this boyo, Jackson, I want a straightforward confession out of him and that'll be an end to it. I've had enough of naked women in bedrooms and all that multi-cultural rubbish. Girl's on the books, I take it? Done any previous?'

'Well, no, sir. She's the wife of a prominent local businessman. Or that's what I've been told.'

'Oh. Right.' Pontin was in no mood thus to be baulked. 'What about *him*?'

'Says he's a university teacher, sir.'

'Christ, now. Drugs, then. That'll be the story. He's been pushing heroin, for a monkey.'

'As yet, sir, we've no evidence—'

'Don't tell *me*, Jackson. I been there before. Flushed it down the loo he has, the crafty dodger. What about the body? Any signs of actual physical torture?'

'I wouldn't go so far as to say that, sir, but then we haven't—'

'Got the murder weapon?'

'Yes, I think so, sir. A typewriter.'

Pontin clicked his tongue. 'The murder *weapon*, Jackson, for God's sake.'

'Yes, sir. A typewriter. Significant blood traces.'

'He hit her over the head with a *typewriter*?'

'That's my present reading of the case, sir.'

'Good God. What are we coming to? What's Paddy Oates got to say about it?'

'Paddy's on holiday, sir. So I called Katie Coyle. That sounds like her arriving now.'

To prevent Dobie from further interfering, however ineffectually, with the progress of police inquiries Jackson had incarcerated him in his study. Pontin found him there, slumped down in his chair at the computer desk; in the grip of some powerful nervous reaction, he was snoring faintly. Pontin shook him briskly by the shoulder, resting his burly frame against the desk; the desk creaked ominously in protest. This complaint Pontin ignored.

'Just a little chat, sir, if you don't mind. Detective-Superintendent Pontin.'

He fixed Dobie with what would have been a cold and level inquisitorial stare if the light from the Anglepoise above the desk hadn't been so strong as to make him blink uncontrollably, causing him to resemble a barn owl repressing a sneezing fit. '. . . Yes, we've met before, I rather fancy. Can't remember what it was I sent you down for, but I never forget a face. And yours is familiar. *Very* familiar.'

What he had in fact for the moment forgotten was Dobie's name. It was a standing grievance with Pontin that the criminals with whom he customarily dealt never had readily memorable names, like Featherstonehaugh or Pontefract. It didn't matter. It would come back to him. 'Wait a second now. Don't tell me . . . *Shoplifting*, that was it, I recall it distinctly. Tacey's Stores? Ladies' knickers? In 1982, wasn't it? I never forget—'

'It was the day before yesterday, actually. At the police station.'

'At the . . . What were you nabbed for?'

'Nothing. I came in to ask you about Sammy Cantwell.'

'What's that got to do with it?'

'Nothing. That's where you saw me before.'

Pontin decided to change tack, as was his frequent strategy when dealing with a slippery witness. Leaning in a confidential manner towards his victim, he adopted an altogether more insidious, avuncular tone. 'Now see here, Mr um ah. I think I should tell you that we've managed to locate the murder weapon. And doubtless there'll be prints. Oh yes, we're pretty sure we'll find plenty of prints. And bearing that in mind, you may feel you'd be well advised to run through your story with me once again. Just for my benefit. Possibly we'll find that you explained it all to Inspector Jackson a little too hurriedly, see? And there may even be a few little points where you'd like to change your . . . Just a few little . . . Wake *up*, will you?'

'Eh?' Dobie said. 'Oh yes. I'm sorry. I really have had a very tiring day.'

'I'm quite sure you have and what I want to know *is*, what that lady is doing without any clothes on in your bedroom.'

Dobie yawned. 'I think it's the gas fire. It makes me doze off.'

Pontin began to speak very slowly and distinctly, in a way that reminded Dobie acutely of Jane herself. 'I want. To know. What that lady. Is doing. In the bedroom.'

'Oh yes. You mean Jane. She isn't doing anything. She's dead.'

'Ah.' Pontin leapt at once upon the cogent point. 'Then you admit. That you know. Who she is?'

Dobie, having yawned cavernously again, began to show some signs of making a spirited recovery. 'Jane? Of course I know Jane. I've known her for years. She's probably my wife's best friend.'

'Then what made you. Decide. To kill her. Sir?'

Dobie saw the trap in time. 'Beg pardon?' he said.

'Someone.' Pontin executed a chopping motion with his right hand. 'Bopter. An accident, perhaps. Was it?'

'Good heavens, no, *I* didn't kill her. She wasn't killed *here*, you know.'

'Not here?'

'No. It was over in *her* house, I saw how it happened. Didn't that other chap tell you? Earlier this . . . There was this burglar with a hat and a raincoat and then he must have brought her over here and put her in my bedroom but I didn't see her because I had this headache and it wasn't until I thought I'd better have an aspirin that I went to get it, you see.'

Throughout this account Pontin had slid himself slowly

back along the full length of the desk, his attitude, moreover, undergoing another subtle change. 'Yes. Yes,' he said nervously. 'I think I've got all that. Excuse me one moment.' Keeping his face turned towards Dobie, he trundled himself back towards the door and beckoned hurriedly to the constable outside. 'Better keep a pretty close eye on this one, Constable. He could be on to us both at the drop of a hat.'

'Yessir. I will, sir,' the constable said.

'He's been under a bit of a strain lately, I shouldn't wonder,' Pontin said, returning to his former position and smiling upon Dobie disarmingly. He was a man who knew his duty and only his glazed-over eyeballs betrayed his inward terror.

'Let's try again, now, shall we? – from a different angle. At least we know you were on friendly terms with the deceased. You've admitted *that*, anyway.'

'Yes. Certainly. So was Jenny.'

'So that gives us a starting point.' Pontin paused. 'Who's Jenny?'

'My wife. She's in Paris.'

'I see. In *Paris*. So you thought while the cat was away—'

This was a mistake. 'What cat?' Dobie said suspiciously. 'I haven't got a cat. Ah. Maybe you're thinking of *Kate*. No, Kate's got nothing to do with it. Except of course she was at the inquest.'

Off again, Pontin thought, glancing cautiously round the room to make sure that no hatchets, chain saws, baseball bats or any other death-dealing weapons were to be seen in the immediate vicinity. 'We haven't had an inquest yet. We've only just found the body. Who's this Kate you're talking about, when she's at home?'

'She isn't at home. She's here. She just *got* here.'

'Ah, she's *here*, is she? Not in Paris?'

'No, no. That was my wife.'

'Who was?'

'The other one. Jenny. She's my wife. The other one isn't. The one in the bedroom. In fact she's somebody else's.'

'Good. It helps, you see, once you've got the background clear. You say your wife has gone to Paris because of this other woman. Now what I want to know—'

'No, wait, you've got that wrong. There *isn't* another woman.'

'Now I understood you quite distinctly to say—'

'I didn't say another woman. I said *the* other woman.'

'That's right. Jenny, you called her.'

'*Now* you've got it. Jenny, my wife. My wife *is* the other woman.'

The sound of Pontin's slow, heavy breathing became clearly audible. 'Perhaps,' he said, 'we'd do better to resume this conversation when you're feeling a little less excited. You seem to have a bit of an attitude problem, if I may say so.'

Meanwhile, Kate was carrying out her preliminary examination.

'Fractured skull all right. Death probably instantaneous. Downward blow from the rear, slightly favouring right hand side. A large flat instrument, something like a brick. No cutting edge. Skin's torn at point of impact but I don't see any minor abrasions. Some blood loss from ears and nose, but not very much. She died too quickly. Okay so far?'

'We know what she was hit with, doctor. What about time of death?'

'Very recent. I'll be checking the rectal temperature in a moment but I'd say some time between nine and nine thirty. She must have died just after taking a hot shower so the skin surface would have been fairly warm. Her hair's still damp, as you noticed. And of course the body's unusually clean, which is rather a pity. From the pathologist's viewpoint, that's to say.'

'We picked up her clothes in the bathroom,' Jackson said. 'And a bath towel from over by that wardrobe. You're not surprising me.'

'She wasn't killed on the bed, of course.'

'No.' Jackson looked down at the scuff marks on the nap of the carpet. 'Probably by the door, as she came in. Nine *thirty*, though? . . . It couldn't have been later?'

He watched Kate take the transparent evidence bags from her medical case and slip them efficiently over the victim's hands. Not a very nice job, he couldn't help thinking, for a woman. Though that was probably old-fashioned prejudice. Pathologists are pathologists, whatever their sex. He looked round as Pontin came in.

'Well?' Pontin said. 'Have we reached a verdict?'

Kate was now gently lifting one of the victim's knees, apparently testing its degree of rigidity. 'Yes. I'll do the autopsy tomorrow morning but there shouldn't be any surprises. Fractured skull is the cause of death. Recently inflicted. A single blow, no other injuries.'

'All right. You can ship her out and we'll get a formal ID at the morgue, soon as we've located the husband. Not much point in asking *him* to do it.' Pontin nodded significantly towards the door. 'Screw loose an' all, if you ask me.'

Jackson adjusted his glasses. 'Are we taking him in, sir?'

'No hurry,' Pontin said. 'No hurry. We should all get our pictures in the paper if we play this right. Got to give the media time to get on the scene, though, see what I mean? It's all public relations nowadays. But we'll finger the bastard in due course, don't you worry.'

'Might be a good idea to let the doctor here take a look at him, don't you think?'

Kate was scrutinising the victim's toes. 'I ought to make it clear,' she said, straightening up, 'that I know Mr Dobie. Personally.'

'Ah,' Pontin said. 'He's a patient of yours already? Can't say I'm surprised.'

'No, I met him . . . He was at an inquest.'

'Ow Gawd, don't *you* start. Just go and feel his pulse or something, soon as you're finished up in here. *Now* what is it?'

This last remark was addressed to Sergeant Evans, who had made a diffident entrance a moment before.

'Just something I thought you'd want to know, sir. We're picking up the deader's prints all over the place – hundreds of them. Along of the owner's, of course.'

'What, here in the bedroom as well?'

'Everywhere,' Evans said. 'And not just new prints neither.'

'Ho ho. So she's been here before tonight?'

'I'd say she's been coming here for *weeks*.'

'What about the murder weapon?'

'Yessir.'

'What d'you mean, yessir?'

'That too, sir. All over the keys. Some of Mr Dobie's on the case and bodywork. No one else's. Just a smudge or two.'

Pontin looked at Jackson. Jackson looked at Pontin.

'We got the bugger bang to rights, then.'

'No, sir.'

'What d'you mean, no sir?'

'There's a snag, sir,' Jackson said. 'According to the doctor's evidence, he couldn't have done it.'

'I don't believe this,' Pontin said.

'He was with me and Detective-Sergeant Box, sir, until half-past nine this evening. Dr Coyle puts the time of death at between nine o'clock and nine thirty. All that time he was ten miles away from here, sir, he was hardly ever out of our sight. Got it all down in my notebook.'

'Jackson?'

'Sir?'

'He's pulled the wool over your eyes somehow. Take my word for it. *That*'s what he's done. About as tricky a witness as I ever encountered. But he did it all right. I can see it in his eyes. That shifty expression of his. You must have noticed it yourself.'

'He certainly seems to be in a state of shock. Hardly in a condition, I'd have thought, to tell us anything useful.'

'Hopes to be found unfit to plead, I've no doubt. I'm not falling for *that* one. No, we'll give him time to consider the error of his ways. Better pack him off home.'

'This *is* his home, sir.'

'Oh yes, well . . . A hotel, then. Or a loony bin. Or something. We can't have him poking around here on the scene of the crime.'

'We haven't a car to spare, sir, not right now.'

'Got his own car, hasn't he?'

'Evans'll need to check it over, sir. And anyway he shouldn't drive, not in his present condition.'

Kate was standing back from the bed now and taking off her surgical gloves. 'I'm going into Cardiff, Mike, when I'm through here. I can drop him off at the Angel or somewhere and save you the trouble.'

'You're not quite through here *yet*, Dr Coyle,' Pontin said bristlingly. 'This matter of the time of death, now. What's all this nonsense about—'

He stopped short as Dobie broke into the room, wild-eyed and brandishing a lady's handbag like something out of *Psycho*. Pontin barely restrained himself from diving incontinently under the bed, which appeared to be high enough to admit his bulk though not, of course, to conceal it. 'Now, now, now, sir,' he said. 'What's all this?' He was aware that his phrasing, however classical in tradition, was notably inadequate to the occasion, but at least it had the effect of bringing Dobie to a shuddery halt.

'That's what *I* want to know,' Dobie said. 'What's *this* doing here?' Flourishing the handbag dramatically aloft. 'Out there in the hallway? What's going *on*?'

Pontin nudged Jackson none too gently in the ribs. 'See what I mean? Get him out of here before he buggers up *all* the evidence . . .'

'This is *Jenny's* bag. My wife's.'

Pontin courageously took a short step forwards. The man had clearly to be disarmed, somehow, as a preliminary measure. 'Now we don't want to go into all that again, do we, sir? You were told to sit down quietly and not touch anything and now here you go—'

'But she took it with her. To Paris. I *know*. I saw her off. How can it—'

He stopped and Jackson saw that his face had become suddenly frozen, his lips drawn right back in a rictus of almost frightening intensity. Everyone was silent. Even Pontin, whose mouth had also opened, didn't speak. Jackson then turned his head to follow the direction of Dobie's petrified gaze, which was obviously riveted on the Medusa-head of the figure on the bed, on the snake-tendrils of fine black hair that wriggled out from it across the pillow. 'Grab him, somebody,' Pontin said, and Jackson got an arm round Dobie's waist just in time to check the impact of his fall.

A white circle spinning on a black screen. A sound as of trickling water. A soothing coolness.

Dobie opened his eyes.

'Come on, Johnno,' Kate said. 'Time to go home.'

He didn't think he had ever felt so tired.

There were stairs, a long flight of them, with Kate's arm helping to push him up them. There was the glow of an electric fire. After a while he stopped shivering. There was coffee, which he drank, and a white pill, which he swallowed. He found then that he was sitting on what felt like a well-sprung bed and Kate was untying his shoelaces, taking off his shoes. '. . . First it was Jane. Then it was Jenny. I don't care what they say.'

'They're confused,' Kate said. 'You can't blame them. So am I.'

'Do they know what happened? Exactly?'

'How do you mean?' She pushed his chest gently and he flopped back on to the mattress like a tipped-over teddy-bear. 'Get your feet up.'

'I mean how was she . . . ?'

'Oh. That. She was hit on the head with a typewriter, it was all very . . . quick.'

'A typewriter. *What* typewriter?'

'The one that was on the table in the bedroom. I'm afraid you may find some of the keys are out of alignment.'

'*I'm* out of alignment,' Dobie said.

'Yes, you are. For the time being.'

'She didn't have any clothes on at all, did she? And Jane did. She had on a black, a black . . . Oh *Jesus*.'

Kate pulled a blanket over him and stooped to tuck the edges in. 'You try and get some sleep. Don't ask yourself too many questions now because the answers won't add up.'

'I can't even get the *questions* to add up.'

'No,' Kate said. 'Perhaps they will later.'

One o'clock in the morning. The ambulance men had been and gone, taking Jenny with them, and Pontin had departed not long afterwards. Constable Pritchett had arrived from Central with a Thermosful of cocoa and, though Jackson could have done with something rather stronger in the way of stimulants, the general atmosphere in Dobie's flat had become a good deal more congenial and relaxed. It was late but the routine was perfectly familiar and Jackson, Box and Evans were carrying it out with the practised ease of old hands.

'They say Mr Corder's in Birmingham. On business. They're not sure if they can locate him,' Box said, cradling the telephone and wiping his hands on his handkerchief. Mercury powder gets everywhere. 'There's a daughter somewhere in Cardiff. They're checking the address.'

'Leave all that to Central, Foxy. This *is* a murder case, not like the other shenanigans. Have some cocoa.'

'One thing's for sure,' Box said, reaching across for the Thermos flask. 'He couldn't have been in two places at the same time.'

'Been a gay day an' all,' Sergeant Evans said. 'Can't remember nothing like it of recent years.'

'*I* can,' Box said. 'DI Connors.'

Jackson said nothing. The sad case of Detective-Inspector Connors was indeed a salutary warning to one and all, and Jackson had reminded himself of it a good deal earlier in the evening. Connors, having been brought to the verge of promotion by the successful prosecution of a subtle and vicious wife-murderer, had been taken considerably aback by the unexpected reappearance upon the scene of the wife in question, the body in the case (which had been discovered in a state of advanced dismemberment) having therefore clearly originally belonged to someone altogether, or anyway distinctively, different. '. . . That's right,' Jackson said eventually. 'You can't be too careful. We got to get a positive identification of the victim before we go much further. I mean, we've only got *his* word for it that it's his wife. Maybe the Supe's right and he's an outright nutter.'

'Prints all over the shop,' Evans said. 'No doubt about that. Like, if she's his wife, that'd account for it.'

'You done that bag yet?'

'Course I have. Same dabs. And of course Mr Dobie's, where the silly bugger went and picked it up.'

Jackson nodded. 'Check it out then, Foxy.'

Box set down his mug of cocoa and reached for the bag. 'Got an airline tag on it all right. *Jennifer Dobie* and the address. CDG . . . What's that?'

'Charles de Gaulle. Paris. I seen all that myself. Get *on* with it.'

Box unzipped the bag and ferreted inside. 'Passport . . .' He glanced inside, flipped it on to the table. 'Photograph checks. So it looks as if it's *her*, right enough. Ticket. Yes, she kept the boarding card . . . Date of flight's been changed. 25th to 24th, that's today. Right. Time of arrival's the same, though. 2045. Quarter to nine.'

'Fits in about right,' Jackson said. 'Assuming the plane got in on time. She'd have got through pretty quickly if that's all the baggage she had. Picked up a taxi . . . How far's the airport from here?'

'Can't be more'n fifteen minutes,' Evans said.

'Say she got here about nine ten or nine fifteen and got under the shower right away, which she might well have done if she'd got a bit wet at the airport . . . And say she was in there about five minutes . . . Looks as though Kate Coyle got it about right. As usual. So then Mr Dobie, of course . . .' Jackson stopped to stare at the brown manila envelope that Box had just extracted from the handbag. 'What you got there?'

'Feels like money,' Box said. He opened the flap of the envelope and let a wad of paper notes slide out on to the table. 'Looks like money.' A big fat wad of hundred-franc banknotes, held together by a rubber band. 'It *is* money. Froggy money at that.'

'Bloody hell,' Jackson said. 'How much have you got *there*?'

'I'll tell you that,' Box said, 'when I've counted it.'

Six o'clock in the morning.

The rains had long since ceased and the skies had partially cleared, though the build-up of cloud to the east was heavy enough to delay the first effect of the sunrise. The sea, sulking, lapped lugubriously at the sand and rocks lying directly beneath the sea-cliffs west of Porthkerry Park, brightening up a little, however, as the tide began to turn and shining rivulets of foam traced out long tentacles between the shallow rock-pools. These and the wet rib-patterns forming on the sodden sand shone brighter and brighter as the sun rose higher and the cloudbanks beyond the Severn Bridge became touched with glowing colour. Mr Jonas Matthias, pensioner and early riser, seemed to detect an unexpected echo of that colour among the jumble of rocks to his left as he strolled, overcoated and gumbooted, across the sands. He changed direction accordingly.

The Home Office expert attendant on the autopsy was Professor Sir Guy Bunter-Coke (better known to junior female members of his staff as Hunter-Poke); when Kate had slit and snipped and probed and forcepped for some forty-five minutes under his kindly supervision and had subsequently refused a dinner invitation for the following Tuesday, Hunter-Poke took his leave and departed, bearing with him various intimate organs subject to more detailed forensic examination. Kate went to the changing-room to scrub her hands and strip off her whites; she wasn't especially surprised when Jackson came in while she was doing this. 'Get any sleep, Inspector?'

'Not very much,' Jackson said. Certainly, his eyes were red behind the rimless lenses.

'Nor did I. And I've got my clinic at ten. You won't get my report till this evening so it's no good your breathing down my neck.'

'I'm afraid they're bringing in another one for you,' Jackson said. 'Fished her out of the sea early this morning. We reckon it's that Mrs Corder but we're not quite sure.'

Kate closed her eyes for a moment as she reached for a towel. '. . . Drowned?'

'That's for you to decide. But I don't think so. Dead before she was pushed in, that's my opinion.'

He watched the neat white hands drying themselves with what seemed to him unnecessary thoroughness.

'Is Paddy Oates still away?'

He nodded. 'For another week yet. Sorry.'

'I'll look at her this afternoon, then. If that's all right.'

'By then we should have a definite ID. You know, the Superintendent's not too happy with your time-of-death estimate on *this* one. You haven't come across anything to make you change your mind?'

'Nothing,' Kate said. She dropped the towel into the disposal bin and looked at her wrist-watch.

'Blue light test?'

'Negative. No sexual activities within the last forty-eight hours. I've got to go.'

She went. Jackson fell into step beside her. Paris, he thought, couldn't be all he'd heard it cracked up to be. 'We're going to need a full statement from your friend Professor Dobie. Should I send a car round for him?'

'All right,' Kate said. 'But not too soon. Can you give him till twelve o'clock?'

'I don't see why not. What sort of shape is he in?'

'I don't know,' Kate said. 'He was still asleep when I left.'

* * *

Throughout the rest of the morning the Barry CID prosecuted their inquiries, aided and abetted by umpteen drafted-in members of the uniformed branch. Patiently and unobtrusively, the spiders of the police force extended their web, with varying degrees, as always, of success. The taxi driver who had taken Jenny from the airport to Dobie's flat was found and questioned, and Interpol were politely requested to check on her movements while in Paris, referring in the first instance to the Agence Azur, the travel agency for which, apparently, she worked. A similar check was inaugurated on Jane Corder's movements throughout the previous day and it was discovered that she had lunched with a Mrs Pretty, co-organiser of a local charitable organisation, at the Cwm Tiddy and had subsequently driven into Cardiff to effect some small purchases at David Morgan; from there she had presumably driven home since her further movements remained, at least for the time being, unaccounted for. Alec Corder had been contacted at a Birmingham hotel and a woman PC had visited Corder Acoustics to advise Wendy of her mother's death, though not (as was considered at this stage tactful) of the surrounding circumstances, while a whole team of conscientious plodders had conducted routine house-to-house inquiries of the occupants of the blocks of flats adjacent to Dobie's, as of the very few houses in proximity to the Corder residence. The typed reports on these investigations already formed a pile five inches high on the Incident Room desk, and Dobie's own lengthy and detailed statement would no doubt be added to them when Superintendent Pontin had finished reading it. This he was doing with incredulity and in the company of Detective-Inspector Jackson, whose eyes were now redder than ever.

'He's sitting there making funny faces at you, Jackson. You realise that?'

'Box is with him in the I Room now, sir. But I don't

think he's going to add anything very material to what we got there.'

Pontin threw the pages of typescript across the desk. This was not the first sign of mild irritation that he had displayed. 'I've never seen such a load of codswallop. Contradicts himself all the bloody time. Hasn't he got a legal adviser? – someone who can get him to talk *sense*?'

'Says he doesn't want one, sir.'

'He wants an alienist, if you ask me.'

This wasn't evident from Dobie's outward appearance. According to the mathematical theories he had earlier advanced to Kate, things only behave in an ordered way between certain limits. Pushed past those limits, they cease to be predictable; thus under the stress of aerial bombardment, for example, born cowards may perform deeds of outright heroism while brave men crack up completely. Dobie, in accordance with this prediction, was being unpredictable. He was, apart from a certain jumpiness, behaving in exactly the same way as he had before, and Box was finding this a little unnerving.

'. . . Exactly fifteen thousand francs, sir. You'll get a receipt for it in due course, naturally. But you made no mention of it in your statement.'

'I didn't know about it,' Dobie said. Placid as you like. 'I'd no idea she had it. I don't know how she got it and I don't know what she planned to do with it. Probably it has something to do with her work at the agency.'

'Well, perhaps the French police will be able to help us there. We do know she was on the Cardiff flight last night and we know she took a taxi to your place and got there at ten past nine.' Sometimes you could get your charley to loosen up by seeming to take him into your confidence. He knew a trick or two, did foxy Boxy. 'It was a radio taxi, luckily enough. So it was all logged. She got a bit wet, though, or so the taxi driver says. So it's natural she'd want to take a nice hot shower as soon as she got back home. Only why should she want to undress in the bathroom? That's where her clothes were.'

'She always did,' Dobie said. 'She didn't like getting undressed in front of me.'

Box, on to him like a flash. 'But you weren't there, sir.'

'She didn't like getting undressed in front of me even when I wasn't there.'

Box sighed heavily. *Exactly* the same as before. A decidedly difficult witness.

'Sort of an old-fashioned girl, was she?'

'I wouldn't say that.'

'What *would* you say then, sir? Can't you tell me anything else about her?'

Dobie thought about this for several seconds.

'Well,' he said. 'She was very fond of peanut butter.'

'. . . A very difficult witness. No doubt about it.'

'The Super thinks he's mental,' Jackson said. 'What's your opinion?'

'I dunno. I just can't get on his wavelength,' Box said. 'But he couldn't have done his old lady in. We're agreed on that much, aren't we?'

'I'll tell you what bothers *me*. Let's suppose the Corder woman *did* die in the way that he's described, no matter how unlikely that may seem. Someone coshed her and pitched her into the drink. Tide took her across the bay and beached her on the turn early in the morning. *That* part of it makes sense, after a fashion.'

'But then she couldn't have turned up dead on his bed, in the way he says.'

'No. I'd've said it was his wife there all the time and the shock of finding her there turned his head somehow. Having the other business on his mind, so to speak. It's pretty wild but it's the only obvious explanation. Okay.

But he also said the woman on the bed was wearing undies. Black undies, right?'

'In fact she wasn't. Just come out of the shower—'

'But this is what they took off the Corder woman when they got her to the morgue. The stuff that's gone to the lab. Here you go.' Jackson selected a flimsy from the paper mountain before him. '*Navy blue Aquascutum raincoat. Cerise cotton blouse*. Sort of a red colour, that is. It's what caught old Matthias' eye when he was walking along the shore this morning. *Black Jaeger slacks. Black flowered satin bra and matching briefs*. Also a couple of rings but they're not to the point. No shoes, but she'd have lost those washing around in the sea. D'you see what I'm getting at?'

'Not quite,' Box said.

'She *was* wearing black underclothes, damn it. But how the hell could *he* have known that? He couldn't, could he? Unless . . .'

'Ah,' Box said. 'Yes. Don't tell me. I've got it.'

It wouldn't be true to say that Pontin's remarks about making funny faces had rankled. Jackson was too used to Pontin's little ways. What was certain was that Dobie's detailed statement, such as it was, constituted an altogether unsatisfactory basis for the kind of investigation that was now under way; it was difficult to check on, no matter how many minions of the law might be devoted to that task, because there was so little to get *hold* of. You had to go for the *facts*, such as they were. When (exactly) Jenny had died, what (exactly) Jane had been wearing. Dobie might or might not be, as Pontin claimed, *non compos mentis* but you can't bring a case to court by guessing at what might or mightn't be going on inside somebody's head. Above all, inside a college professor's head. An odd crowd, that lot.

And Dobie, it had to be admitted, was odder than most.

* * *

In Dobie's flat, everything was somehow different. The police had tidied up scrupulously after their examination, but that in a way was the trouble; it was *too* tidy. It was no longer a flat but a scene-of-crime, a museum exhibit. An exhibit that Dobie didn't much want to see. He stood, therefore, at his sitting-room window, looking out across the street, at the blocks of flats opposite and at the shadowy hills beyond Radyr, just visible between them. Saturday afternoon. Everything was quiet. Except for the thump of pop music, echoing from the open windows of a neighbouring flat; an unidentifiable disco number, a high-pitched female voice yowling plaintively, repetitively into an inattentive emptiness. Every now and again a car passed by. Behind the hills the sky was almost clear of cloud but devoid of colour, washed out by last night's rain. Within the flat the heat of summer had returned, heavy and a shade oppressive, and Dobie thought that he could hear, behind the emphatic beat of the music and the anguished wails of Sinitta or whoever it was, a quieter yet equally insistent female voice carolling tunelessly away in another room somewhere. Nearer, yet infinitely further away. Odd to think how the grating inaccuracy of that other voice had come close, at times, to driving him round the twist. But then there seemed to be quite a few things that he'd do best not to think about. Or not yet, anyway.

Mathematics is basically a frame of mind. A habit of economy of thought. What he had to acquire now, and very quickly, was a habit of economy of emotion. To discard all those feelings that he didn't really feel and concentrate his mind upon the genuine element in his loss, as he might have done if his arm, say, had been amputated. Because in one way it wasn't as bad as *that.* In another way, it was worse. Something you had, in any case, to come to terms with. Because there was no workable alternative.

Kate also seemed to have a habit of economy. Economy of movement. She had been sitting behind him for the past ten minutes without moving, without saying anything, motionless yet apparently quite relaxed. In the end Dobie turned away from the window and sat down opposite her and for a few moments longer they stared at each other in silence.

'You look like *shit*,' Kate said.

'That's the way I feel. Three hours they had me in that police station,' Dobie said. 'Three hours and a bit. It was tiring.'

'You should have had your lawyer along. Don't you have one?'

'It'd be just one more person I'd have to explain it all to and I'm tired of it. Like I said.'

'Well, who's your doctor?'

'I don't have one. I'm never ill. You know,' Dobie said, 'I told them everything that happened, every damned thing, and I don't think they believed a word of it. I'm not sure that I can blame them.'

'Perhaps they believe a bit more now than they did last night. Did they tell you they found Jane Corder?'

Dobie closed his eyes for a moment. 'They didn't tell me anything about that.'

'Washed up on the beach. This morning.'

'It happened like I said it did,' Dobie said.

'Would you like me to make you some tea? Or coffee? Or maybe pour you something out of a bottle?'

'Not unless *you*'d like something.'

'You haven't killed anybody.'

'Of course not. Why would I have?'

'Jackson can't see any reason why you should have. That's probably why you're not still at the station. Detained in custody. *I* shan't tell him anything.'

'About what?'

'About Jenny. You told me she was having an affair.'

'Even if she were,' Dobie said, 'that wouldn't be a reason for me to—'

'Some people might think so. Pontin might. But that isn't the real point.'

'What *is* the real point?'

'. . . That if you didn't kill her, someone else did.'

Dobie looked again towards the window. 'Someone else did,' he agreed.

'You must have *some* idea who she was seeing.'

'I haven't,' Dobie said. 'At one time I thought I might have, but it turned out I was wrong. You see . . . I didn't really want to know. Can you understand that?'

'Yes. And I suppose that makes you feel guiltier than ever.'

'I don't know that I do,' Dobie said. Economy of emotion, that was the ticket. Certain feelings now were luxuries he couldn't afford, and what Kate was talking about was one of them. 'It doesn't seem to matter very much. Not now.'

'You shouldn't stay here, you know.'

'I think I ought to.'

'Why?'

'I've been running away from things for long enough.'

The sunlight, angling in through the window, formed a pool of brightness around Kate's neat legs, neat shoes, neatly folded skirt. Her face, still turned towards him, remained in the shadows. 'There are things that *any* sensible person would want to run away from. Things like newspaper people. Journalists. The TV news crowd. All that lot.'

'Surely they won't be very interested—'

'Dobie, for God's sake be your *age*. They'll be camping down outside this place any moment. All the tabloids have their police contacts, you know, it's a wonder they didn't catch you when you left the station. And when they do, it'll be *worse* than murder, believe you me.'

Dobie thought that this might well be true. It was a consideration that hadn't occurred to him until that moment. 'But where would I *go*? There isn't anywhere—'

'You can stay in Sammy's room, if you like. It won't be so easy for them to find you there. I know it's not very luxurious, but it'll do for the time being.'

'Are you sure that'll be all right?'

'It will be as soon as I've got it ready. Clean sheets and so on.' She got to her feet. 'Pack a few things, get in your car and drive round there now. Don't hang around any longer than you can help.'

She turned and was gone, before Dobie could offer to see her to the door. Economy of effort, yes, but when Kate moved she *moved*. Decisiveness is sometimes contagious; Dobie hurried into his study and got down his own weekend bag from the shelf, shovelled into it his work file, a box of mini-discs and the package from MIT. What else did he need? . . . Clothes, of course.

He hesitated for a few moments, his fingers clenched round the handle of his bag. Then he picked it up and went through to the bedroom. Spare suit, a couple of shirts, a few pairs of socks, pyjamas, his dressing-gown. Like going up to town for a conference, really. Nothing to it. His spongebag was in the bathroom. He fetched it. Now. Was that the lot? . . . Maybe the typewriter would come in useful. He went to fetch . . .

Yes. That was *really* silly.

He found that he'd started trembling again. Not shivering, but trembling. He couldn't hold his hands steady. He'd had enough. He grabbed the holdall and walked down the hallway, head up, breathing deeply, slowly. Outside, he felt a little better. He unlocked the door of the Fiesta and got in.

He had the sensation that several hundred pairs of beady eyes were fixed upon him from behind drawn curtains as he drove away. Yes, that was silly, too.

But Kate's reference to the potential marauding activities of the tabloid journalists had disturbed him. Even during the three and a quarter hours he had spent at his friendly local cop shop, he had been aware only of the distressing extent of his personal involvement; it hadn't occurred to him to see himself as the centre of an enormous palpitating circle of breathless interest and intrigue, a circle within whose outer rim hundreds, if not thousands, of his fellow-citizens would be included. As the key witness, in short, of a Murder Case. As virtually the instigator of a complex problem towards the elucidation of which the most earnest efforts of whole battalions of his country's police force, supplemented by the eagerly baying hounds of the mass media and by the cooperation of a substantial cross-section of the general public, might well soon be devoted. He hadn't seen it from that point of view at all.

This was because he hadn't seen the problem itself in that sort of a light. It just didn't look to be that *kind* of a problem, the kind that might be eventually unravelled through faithful adherence to an established routine; you might as well ask the police, the journalists and the men-in-the-street to determine the square root of minus one. There was something like a strange attractor at work, way way back behind the scene, an entity that would only reveal itself to a different mode of inquiry, to a creative imagination. A mathematical imagination. To an element that the police investigators lacked. If their interrogation methods were anything to go by. They hadn't believed a word of it, not a word . . .

Though here Dobie was doing the bogeys rather less than justice. Foxy Boxy? . . . No mathematician, he. But the nickname implied, at least, the possession of a certain imagination, if of a limited kind. Low cunning, some might call it.

'. . . *Strangers on a Train*,' Box was, at that very

moment, saying. 'Good film, that. Jevver see it?'

Jackson wasn't much of a one for film-going and levelled on his subordinate a stare of disfavour. His eyes were now so inflamed from continuous concentration upon reading matter that his expression in itself might have guaranteed him a starring role in a Hammer horror movie; hairs seemed to be about to sprout from his otherwise unremarkable features at any moment. 'Save the chitchat for later, Foxy, or we'll never get through.'

'No, look, there's these two geezers, see? and they fix it so each one of them does the other one's murder for him. 'Cause that way they both have alibis. It's clever. Suppose this Dobie feller was to knock off another bloke's old lady while the other bloke got rid of *his* wife for him . . . See what I mean?'

Jackson thought that he did, but wasn't impressed. 'A bit far-fetched, though, innit?'

'I dunno. It says here that Dobie and the Corder woman's husband were college students together. And it all seems to me like the kind of thing a couple of college kids might dream up, being that way inclined. Ingenious, like. Mind you, that was another one. *Rope*. They put the body in a chest and sat on it.'

Jackson looked at his wrist-watch. 'Well, you're due to meet Mr Corder at the city morgue in half an hour's time. Keep an eye on him when he does the ID and if he tries to sit on top of the corpse, let's know about it.'

'You will have your little joke,' Box said unresentfully.

He himself had thought his suggestion to be a bit far out. Jackson, however, pushed back his chair and didn't resume his reading until some time after Box had gone.

Once you'd met Alec Corder, the suggestion seemed further out than ever. Corder wasn't the kind of man who would readily delegate responsibility, certainly not for so simple a matter as bumping off an unwanted wife or two. As for identifying the victim once the deed was performed, that was like stealing an infant's sucker. Corder marched unhesitantly up to the besheeted figure on the trolley, the morgue assistant expertly flicked the sheet back, Corder gave a brief but emphatic nod of acknowledgement, the assistant flicked the sheet back again and that was it. Box was fully prepared to wait respectfully for a few moments while Corder turned his face to the wall in manly sorrow, but Corder instead swung abruptly around and was on to him like a rabbit on to a parsnip. '. . . Right. Who's in charge of this case? Pontin?'

'Detective-Superintendent Pontin, yes, sir.'

'I want to know a great deal more about it than I do right now,' Corder said, snapping an elbow lock on to Box's right arm and marching him relentlessly out into the hollowly echoing corridor. 'And if he's not prepared to talk to me about it, then I know just the fellow to see and it *is* the Chief Constable I have in mind. I'd be obliged if you'd make that clear to him.'

'I'm sure the Superintendent will be pleased to see you, sir, as soon as we've received the autopsy report. And if in the meantime you'd care to come round to the station and make a short statement—'

'One thing I can tell you for a start,' Corder said, steering Box effortlessly round a corner. 'There's no way at all she could have fallen in. She was always scared of the sea. Couldn't swim a stroke.'

'We don't think she was drowned, sir. We've every reason to suppose her death wasn't natural. I don't think I should say any more than that, at this stage.'

Corder's grip on his elbow tightened, though no more than momentarily. 'What are you implying, exactly?'

'All we want at the moment is to establish an identification, sir. I don't wish to imply *anything*.'

'Not your place to do so, no doubt.'

'That's it, sir.'

'Then we'll see what your Superintendent has to say. You've got your identification. That was Jane all right.'

They left the side entrance and headed for the car park, in this way crossing the path of Dr Caitlin Coyle who was moving in some haste in the obverse direction. Her immediate destination was the autopsy room, where the dissection trolley had already arrived and old Hunter-Poke was already walking abstractedly up and down with his hands interlaced behind his back, a style of locomotion which in his (totally mistaken) opinion accentuated his overall resemblance to the Duke of Edinburgh. 'Ah, so here you are. Never a dull moment, eh, m'dear?'

'Good evening, Sir Guy. I hope I'm not late.'

'Ah, that's the nice thing about corpses. They usually wait.' Emitting a sinister cackle redolent of advanced senility, Hunter-Poke advanced avariciously upon the cadaver. 'A nice well-nourished one for you today. Bet she cuts up lovely.'

'You'd like me to carry out the dissection again?'

'Oh, I think so, don't you? My old hands aren't as steady as once they were.' Hunter-Poke illustrated this contention by poking the late Mrs Corder in the ribs with a quivering index finger. 'Picked her out of the sea, did they now? Well, she didn't drown. That's obvious.'

Kate, in her turn, moved forwards to scrutinise the palely upturned face. 'I think I've seen her somewhere before.'

'Local lady, isn't it? You could have done.' Hunter-Poke pushed the head slightly sideways while Kate was still staring down at the face. 'She took a bit of a knock before she went in, as you can see. Unless she picked it up on the way down.'

'Well, we're not here to make guesses, are we?' Kate said. 'I'll get washed up and do the prep if it's all right with you.'

'Oh, carry on by all means, dear lady,' Hunter-Poke said.

Pathologists are rarely very good cooks, but mathematicians are worse. Between them they managed well enough, however, chiefly by reading and following the instructions on the back of the frozen food packet, and Dobie found the atmosphere of Kate's small kitchen, now doing additional service as a temporary dining room, restful and congenial. And also neat and clean, which made for a change. There was a huge Aga cooker which made contented bubbling sounds, saucepan things were hung on convenient wall hooks (so that one didn't have to stoop down to put them into cupboards, cracking one's head on the shelving in the process) and hot water gushed copiously from the taps. An old-fashioned kitchen, you might say, devoid of almost all modern inconveniences. The beef stew they ate sensibly with soup spoons – a procedure that Jenny had always regarded as being vulgar – and, as it tasted rather nice, they mopped up the remnants from the plates with pieces of bread. Kate, for all her slender not to say skinny frame, clearly had a man-sized appetite. 'It's being so cheerful,' she said, 'as keeps me going. But food helps, there's no denying it.'

'Doing autopsies doesn't seem to put you off. I think it would me.'

'Not when you'd got used to it.'

'You've done a lot?'

'Not all that many. It's only a part-time thing, really. They call me in when no one else is available, but that happens more often than you might think. The truth of the matter is, I need the wonga. I haven't got all that big a practice here, I might do better if I had a partner.'

'Surely if the practice isn't very big—'

'A *male* partner. Lots of people still don't like woman doctors, you know. At least corpses don't have prejudices, or if they do they don't show them.' Kate helped herself to a slice of the enormous slab of Cheddar that stood on the table and bit into it with small shark-like teeth. '. . . I've seen her somewhere before, you know. I'm sure of it.'

'Who?'

'Your friend. Mrs Corder.'

'She's been living here these past twenty-five years,' Dobie said. 'You could have done. Or maybe seen her picture in the papers.'

'What papers?'

'The local ones. She did a lot of charity work. Giving prizes at flower shows and so forth.'

'Rich, was she?'

'Alec is. *And* successful.'

'I just caught a glimpse of him today. I didn't take to him much. But it must be nice.'

'What must be nice?'

'To be rich and successful.'

Dobie watched her munch away at the cheese. Her face, he thought, was a little too wide in proportion to its length and, as she ate, small muscles flexed under the cheekbones. She looked like a rather energetic cat enjoying a breakfast canary. He said, 'It can't be a coincidence, can it? . . . Their both getting killed like that. There has to be *some* connection.'

'You said they were friends.'

'I meant some *outside* connection. And then again, Sammy Cantwell . . .'

'Sammy worked for Corders.'

'Yes.'

'But there's no other connection, is there?'

'Not that I know of.'

Leaning back and stretching out a hand, Kate could switch on the electric coffee percolator without getting up from the table. She did so.

'When you first went into that bedroom,' she said,

'you thought it was Jane Corder lying on the bed. When really it was Jenny. How could you have possibly made a mistake like that? They weren't the least bit alike.'

'I didn't make a mistake,' Dobie said. 'It *was* Jane Corder.'

'She was in the sea by then. Just like you said.'

'I never said she was in the sea. Jackson inferred that she was from what I told him, and even then I don't think he fully believed it until she was actually found there. But she *wasn't* in the sea. She was in my bedroom. Or she was at around ten o'clock that night.'

'I'll tell you one thing,' Kate said. 'She wasn't drowned. She died in the same way as Jenny, except that the blow was upward instead of downward and landed lower down, just above the base of her neck. *Then* she was pushed into the sea. It could have happened exactly as you said. Except, of course, *you* could have done it. You were there in the house. And all that stuff about a burglar . . . You could have made it up.'

'I know,' Dobie said.

'But then you couldn't possibly have done them *both*. And Jackson probably can't decide which one of the two to nab you for.'

Dobie was alarmed. 'You mean . . . *arrest* me? My God, I hope he doesn't do *that*.'

Kate disconnected the percolator and lifted it over to the table, almost but not quite overbalancing her chair backwards in the process. 'Dobie, there has to be someone up there who *likes* you. I mean, your presence here is the strongest argument for the existence of a deity I've ever come across.'

'Oh,' Dobie said. 'That's your considered medical opinion, is it?'

'Not really. As a doctor, I don't have any views on theology. But then I can't be a doctor *all* the time. I have my likes and dislikes. And intuitions. For instance, I don't take much to your Jenny, either.'

'You never knew her.'

'Exactly.'

Saturday night after-dinner conversation, Dobie thought. As on so many previous occasions with the Traynors or the Wains or eating out now and then at the Trattoria or the Park Hotel or that Chinese place. Intuitions and their rôle in mathematical research. Whether God could abrogate the laws of syllogism. Whether Gorbachev would change the rules of the Russian rat-race. Tobacco smoke, black coffee and brandy. Pleasant and even sometimes stimulating. All the ingredients here, except that they weren't dressed for it; he jacketless and tieless, Kate in some loose kind of a housecoat thing, a caftan, maybe. But no. This was different. In one way, this was unreal. In another way, it was all those other after-dinner conversations that now seemed to be unreal and always had been. '. . . I probably didn't, either,' Dobie said.

'Did you think you did? At one time?'

'We never really knew each other at all. But that, you see, seemed to make it more . . . exciting. Probably when we first met we found each other a bit overpowering, I'd never met anyone like her and I don't think she'd met very many people like me. So . . . Well. There you go.'

'What was unusual about her?'

'I don't quite know,' Dobie said. '*Something* was.'

'I don't have to ask that question of you,' Kate said. 'You really are some kind of weird. An awful lot of women find that attractive. And then you're sort of *uncouth*, physically. I mean, a smoothie you're not. I can quite see that you might have a certain appeal.'

'Maybe. But that was where it seemed to go all wrong.'

'The sexual side of it?'

'Yes. No, well, we *did* it, I don't mean that. But

she just didn't seem to *enjoy* it much, is all. She'd sort of . . .'

'Close her eyes and think of England?'

'Somewhere a good deal further away than that. Outer Siberia, maybe. To judge by the results.'

'You didn't ask anyone for advice?'

'What sort of advice?'

'A marriage counsellor or someone like that?'

'No,' Dobie said. 'I thought maybe things would get better. But they didn't. And Jenny never seemed to . . . It was as though she thought *all* marriages were like that.'

'Probably more of them are than you might suppose. More coffee?'

Dobie pushed his mug across the table. 'That's why I found it hard to believe, when I got the idea she might be seeing someone else. Or hard to *imagine*.'

'She wasn't with anyone else,' Kate said, 'while she was in Paris. Not in the way you mean. The way we're talking about. If you thought she was.'

Dobie was silent for a moment, gazing at the percolator as she tilted it over the mug. 'You can . . . *tell* about things like that?'

'Yes. You can. What gave you the idea? – in the first place?'

'There wasn't a first place. I mean there wasn't a specific moment when I suddenly realised . . . Nothing like *that*. I suppose it was just a sort of a change in her attitude. Not towards me. Towards things in general. About three months ago, it started. I thought it was a change for the better, at first, because she seemed a lot more . . . light-hearted. Always *singing* round the place. Off-key. It was driving me nearly bonkers.'

'And you took that to be a side-effect of infidelity.'

'No. Of course not.' Dobie made an exasperated gesture that endangered the security of his newly-replenished coffee mug. 'It's hard to . . . There were lots of little things. Things she was secretive about. She hadn't been that way before. That business about the money, for instance – you know about the money? . . . She brought back from France? *I* didn't know anything about it when they asked me. I felt a bit of a twit, in fact. Not knowing. And then there was the wig . . .'

'The *wig*?'

'Fluffy blonde thing, I couldn't make out . . . I only found it one day by accident because she kept it hidden away in one of her bedroom drawers. I wouldn't have *minded* her wearing a wig, why ever should I? But I couldn't ask her about it, either, she might have thought I'd been . . . nosing around. Or something.'

'I think in your place,' Kate said, 'I'd have been more worried about weekends in Paris than about that sort of thing. It seems pretty trivial.'

'Yes, but a trip to Paris at least is *explicable*. The other isn't.'

'Had she been there before?'

'Oh yes. She has a summer job with a French travel firm, she has to go there for briefings and so on. This was, let's see . . . her third trip since she . . . Since the end of May, I think. This time she could have drawn some advance pay or something like that. But again, why should she have?'

'Perhaps she meant to give you a surprise.'

'I got that, all right,' Dobie said.

Some kind of disloyalty had to be involved in discussing his marital problems in this way; it was something, as he himself had just admitted, that he'd never done before. But Jenny was dead. That made a difference. His pretensions to loyalty, to her memory or whatever, were also a part of that vaguely emotional baggage which had encumbered him for so long and which her death made it necessary for him to discard. Because if I do that, Dobie thought, maybe I *can* get to know her, after all. Knowledge may come too late and still be important. Talking like this to Kate may make it all a bit easier, but it's only a step along the way. He blinked ponderously, ladling sugar into his coffee, seeing the road stretch out ahead of him, stony, dusty, dangerous. Perhaps this evening was one he'd remember in the distant future. You never can tell.

'What about you, Kate?'

'Me?'

'You wear a wedding ring.'

'Oh, that.' She looked down at her hand almost as though in surprise. 'Well, the other Dr Coyle's with an oil company somewhere in the Middle East and it's a good long while since anyone inquired after him. And when they do, that's about all I can tell them. We're not in touch. If we ever were.'

'He's a doctor, too?'

'He is that.'

'You said something earlier on about wanting a male partner.'

'I didn't mean it. Yes, that was the whole idea when we were both students. It wasn't a good idea. It didn't work out. I think we were probably sold on the idea more than on each other. And that was the trouble. Stupidity.'

'The work still has to be done,' Dobie said, 'whether you do it together or not.'

'That's very true.'

'It's there to do and so you get on with it. It's like that with me. I don't know if it's a good thing but it's something that I'm good *at*. Whether it's *enough* . . . That's another matter.'

'It is if it has to be.'

'I'm not sure about that.'

The telephone rang in the next room and Kate went

to answer it. While she was gone, Dobie golloped his coffee reflectively and wondered if he was really sure that he wasn't sure. Because what he did wasn't *work*, exactly. Teaching was work, despite what some people said. The patterns that formed on his monitor screen were something else. There because he formed them first in his mind. Created them. Out of nothing. Not work but a feeling. The only feeling he could now allow himself. Kate wasn't gone very long.

'It's for you.'

'For me?'

'Pontin. He wants to speak to you.'

Dobie got up with a certain reluctance and went to the telephone. In fact it wasn't Pontin. It was Alec Corder.

'Alec? I thought it was . . . Alec, I'm terribly sorry, this about Jane . . .'

There were rattling noises and a sound of voices in the background. The call, no doubt, was coming through from Pontin's office, where Corder would by now as a matter of course have assumed command. '. . . Well, we're both in the same boat, aren't we?' Corder was saying. 'Far as that goes. Anyway, I've been on to the Chief Constable and he's promised me he's really going to get things moving on this one, so we can set our minds at rest on *that* score. Meantime I think we ought to get together and talk things over, what d'you say?'

'Yes, I think we should,' Dobie said. 'But it's a bit late tonight. How about—'

'No, no, not *tonight*, I've had a hell of a day and I imagine you have, too. Can we say tomorrow morning? At my place? Any time to suit you?'

'All right,' Dobie said.

'Good. Elevenish, then. Bloody business, this, any way you look at it, and worse for you than for me in some ways. From all accounts. But we'll talk about all that tomorrow.'

'I'll be there.'

The telephone clicked in Dobie's ear and he looked at it for a moment before replacing it on its cradle. He'd expected to hear from Alec but not quite so soon. But then he hadn't allowed for Alec's manic energy; it went without saying that he didn't share it. Unenergetically, he lumbered back to the kitchen, where Kate was finishing the washing-up. 'I was going to give you a hand with that,' Dobie said, not very convincingly.

'Not to worry. It's finished.' She was indeed in the act of removing her dinky apron. 'I could do with an early night and so could you. Sunday tomorrow, thank heaven.'

'That was Alec Corder on the buzzer. I said I'd run over and see him in the morning.'

'Back for lunch?'

'Yes. Or I would think so. But I can't very well—'

'That's okay. I'll fix up something. And if you could manage to keep out of trouble between now and next nosh-time, I'd be much obliged. I know it's asking a hell of a lot—'

'What sort of trouble could I possibly get into?'

'Oh Christ,' Kate said. 'You name it.'

Sammy's room. But Dobie's room, now. The bed neatly made, Dobie's weekend bag resting at its foot. The computer on the work-table showing its keys to him in a welcoming smile, recognising a computer-friendly occupant. The room seemed a little dark after the French-windowed and airy lightness of Dobie's own bedroom, but not at all gloomy; more like a burrow, a secure recess of some deep warren where a weary rabbit might rest its limbs safe from the scrabbling paws of pursuing terriers. A place where Dobie's special form of work might be prosecuted in peace and relative quiet. His student digs hadn't been so very different.

And Cantwell, too, perhaps a kindred spirit. With his A grade in mathematics, his computer software programmed to handle Lorenzian equations. Dobie wondered if he'd thought to bring the Mandelstam set to bear on the isolation problem; it was something he could check on later. Cantwell was dead now, but not completely gone. His work was there, could be carried on; his bed was there, and could be slept in. An early night. Why not?

The holdall was there, too, of course, and Dobie's pyjamas were in it. He put it on the bed and unpacked it. George Campbell's programmes and the mini-discs went on to the work-table; his spare suit . . . Dobie opened the wardrobe. Sammy Cantwell's clothes still hung there, but there was plenty of room for one suit more. One suit more. One suit more . . .

Alongside that grey belted raincoat . . .

On the shelf above the raincoat, a slightly flattened pork-pie hat . . .

Instead of putting away the suit, Dobie took out the raincoat and turned it round. There had, of course, to be hundreds like it. Probably thousands. This one had a little name-tag inside the collar with *S. Cantwell* written on it in marking ink. Dobie felt in the pockets. They were empty except for a crumpled sheet of paper. The paper had words written on it, too. Dobie stared at it uncomprehendingly.

BACK SOON PLEASE GO IN MAKE YOURSELF AT HOME

. . . Or not written but typed. In red. With a purple squiggle underneath. Dobie sat down on the bed, holding the sheet of paper in his hand.

Someone else, he thought, was making patterns in his mind. Creating them out of nothing. Someone was being very creative indeed.

3

Church bells ringing. Ding dong bell. On the pavement leading up to St Joseph's the Sunday cohorts were walking, soberly dressed, wearing industrious expressions. The morning sun shone brightly on grey stone, yew trees, well-trimmed green lawns. The rains had had a freshening effect on the grass, the summer leaves, even on the granite gravestones outside the church, which had a freshly-washed look about them. Dobie was freshly washed and shaved but not noticeably freshened. He drove on down the street, cautiously slowing down for the road junction and the little cluster of shops around it where incautious pedestrians, emerging from the newsagents with their noses in the *News of the World* and their heads as often as not still aching from the sociable excesses of Saturday night, were wont to step blithely off the pavement and vanish between the wheels of intemperately-conducted vehicles. All these disco places, Dobie thought crossly. They have a mind-numbing effect. Glancing sideways as he passed the shops, he perceived outside the newspaper emporium a very large placard bearing the announcement,

CARDIFF WOMEN VICTIMS IN DOUBLE SEX MURDER

The wording of this message had an even more spectacularly mind-numbing effect on him and on entering the main road he only narrowly avoided running over a middle-aged lady pushing a perambulator who, having emitted a penetrating squeak, was just able to seek refuge on the central island in the nick of time. Dobie, shaken by this encounter and redoubling his concentration, continued on his journey. The Corder residence, when he arrived there some fifteen minutes later, seemed to be doing even better business than St Joseph's; a considerable crowd of some thirty or forty loiterers had apparently taken root on the strip of pavement outside the front gate, a TV-news van was prominently parked some ten feet distant and a uniformed policeman was providing a non-nuclear but determined deterrent to those avid sensation-seekers who were attempting to gain admission to the property itself. Dobie was relieved to find himself recognised at once and waved benignly through; the three-and-a-quarter hours he had spent at the police station the day before had clearly not been altogether in vain. What with one thing and another, though, it had been a nerve-racking drive and, once safely within the house and seated once again in the front room, he was even more relieved to be greeted with the sweetest words of thought or pen or with what might, anyway in the circumstances, be so regarded.

'Not too early for you, is it?'

'No, indeed not,' Dobie said.

The whisky bottle in Alec's sturdy hands made musical noises and Wendy, who had been gazing glumly out of the front window at the goings-on outside, came to plump herself ganglingly down on the sofa beside them. 'Those people. They're not going to go away.'

'We'll see about that,' Corder said grimly.

'You'll just have to get used to it, Daddy. The policeman *did* warn you.'

Dobie could understand their perturbation. You didn't have to look out of the window to be aware of that lurking presence outside, not in the least threatening but docilely inquisitive, like the audience at an Alan Ayckbourn play intent upon watching other people going quietly bonkers, bored wives and unassuming husbands being pushed to the ends of their respective tethers. The house itself was a little too much like a stage, its furniture a little too unused and a little too carefully arranged; Dobie had always thought so, but he also knew that the houses of most wealthy people were like this. Perhaps they wouldn't feel comfortable if things were otherwise.

'What I can't make out,' Corder said, 'is what they expect to *see*.' He raised his laden glass vaguely in Dobie's direction. 'Oh well. She's right, of course. Daughters usually are, you know. It's a most annoying habit of theirs.'

'Not true,' Wendy said. 'I wish it were.'

This morning she was wearing sky-blue knee-length shorts and a yellow rollneck pullover and wasn't looking at all secretarial. She looked sort of Home-Counties and *horsy*, Dobie thought, which was odd because to the best of his knowledge she didn't ride at all. But then his knowledge didn't amount to very much. Her last remark seemed to have irritated her father slightly and Dobie couldn't see why. 'All right – now that *this* has happened I'm sure we both wish things had worked out rather differently. But it's no good letting your mind dwell on it. Business as usual and carry on regardless. That's the ticket.'

'I'm *not* dwelling on it. I didn't mean that at all.'

Corder stared down at the whisky swirling restlessly around in his tumbler. 'Let's take these into my study, shall we, John? Those bloody people out there, they're getting on my nerves.'

Corder's study at least faced the other way; nothing could be seen through the picture window but a blue-grey expanse of shifting sea and the shapes of a few distant merchant ships lying off Sully Roads. A desk and a shelfload of red-bound books seemed to be there chiefly in order to justify its description; it wasn't study-like in any other sense and Corder appeared to be aware of this, to the point of feeling a need to apologise for it. '. . . Never much liked this place, to tell you the truth. Never did. Nor does Wendy, really.'

'I gather she doesn't live here any more.'

'No,' Corder said, giving a leather-backed armchair quite a vicious kick before turning and sitting down on it. 'Not since she started working with us. I found her a nice little room in Fairwater, right above the shop, so to speak. Well, a five-minute drive, anyway. Jane made a hell of a fuss at the time but you know what mothers are like. Or you can imagine it, anyway.'

'Jane made a fuss about most things.'

'So she did. Still, the kid wanted to be independent, the way kids do, and I could see her point of view. Anyway, I'm all for peace and quiet. Aren't you?'

'Very much so.'

'Yes,' Corder said. 'Ironical, that.'

He stared down again into his whisky glass, holding it cupped in both hands. It was a pose of deep despondency, but not a studied one. It was probably true that he'd never liked the house; the house was Jane's choice, and all its furnishings, and now that she was gone he had to feel himself, in a strange way, to be on foreign territory. Even here. Even in his study. '. . . I suppose,' he said, 'I'd better hear all about it. That's if you feel like telling me.'

Dobie didn't, not really, but it was something that had to be done. Yet again. With the coherence developed of practice, he went through his story and Alec listened to it. Since at no point did Alec show any obvious signs of surprise, Dobie deduced that he'd heard most of it already, probably from Pontin. But the story admittedly did seem to sound a little more extraordinary each time he told it. '. . . That's what *happened*, though, Alec. And I haven't held anything back. I'd have no reason to.'

'Funny about Jane's not being here when you arrived, if that was what you'd arranged. Most unlike her.'

'That's what I thought at the time. But—'

'And you've no idea what it was she wanted to talk to you about?'

'None at all. Unless maybe it had something to do with Jenny. But that doesn't make much sense, either. Jane wouldn't have told me anything bad about Jenny, it wouldn't have been . . . *loyal*.'

'Why would it need to be something bad?'

'Isn't it usually?'

Corder shook his head, but not in disagreement. 'Yes. With women, I suppose it usually is. That note she left . . . You've given it to the police?'

'Not yet. I've got it here in my pocket, as a matter of fact.'

'Could I see it?'

Dobie handed it over and Corder read it. Several times.

'. . . Well, it's her typewriter all right. Red part of the ribbon because the switch got jammed. I was wondering if . . .'

'Yes,' Dobie said. 'Anyone could have put it there.'

'But not anyone could have written it.'

'Jane could have written it but at some other time.'

'Well, yes.' Corder shook his head again and returned the note to Dobie. 'You've been doing some thinking about it, obviously.'

'Of course I have.'

'Me, too. Are you *going* to give it to the police?'

'No,' Dobie said.

'No. All right. I shan't mention it. All the same . . . Yes, Pontin's an idiot, but when all's said and done the police are professionals. I'm not sure we'd be wise to get mixed up in this thing ourselves.'

'I *am* mixed up in it,' Dobie said.

'Any more than you are already, I mean.'

'The trouble is, I know one thing that they don't.'

'What's that?'

'That I didn't do it.'

'Good God. Are you *serious*?'

'Very.'

'They couldn't possibly believe it was *you* who . . . ?'

'They not only could, I think they *do*.'

'But that's ridiculous. I've known you for thirty years. It's the most preposterous . . . Yes. I see what you mean.'

The glass of the picture window vibrating gently. Corder ignoring the sound, Dobie looking up. The whine of jet engines, growing louder and louder. From other, rounded windows the passengers would be looking downwards at the house and the people outside it and the line of the beach and the grey rocks and the smooth unruffled surface of the sea. Under that unruffled surface, the abyss. The nothingness of infinity. Once again, Dobie felt fear.

Corder wasn't altogether ignoring that sound, after all. It was too loud, too penetrating to be ignored. 'Bloody aircraft,' he said. 'I think I'll get rid of this place. I'm starting to *hate* it.'

Outside the house. Outside the church. Only three days ago Dobie had been like that himself, one of that numberless multitude soberly going about their daily business, talking to students, conferring with colleagues, walking quietly from staff room to lecture hall, upstairs, downstairs, work work work, and treading all the time on that glass-fine crust holding them all briefly up from nothing. A crust as thin as a sheet of paper pinned to a door that opened, again, on nothing. No, he wouldn't show that paper to the police. They wouldn't understand. Alec wouldn't, either.

'It's like this every day in the summer. Paris flight

coming over. Twice every day we have to put up with it, taking off and landing. It doesn't worry me as much as it might,' Corder said, 'I'm always at the office, but I've complained about it all the same. Jane's complained. Doesn't do a blind bit of good.'

'No,' Dobie said. 'It doesn't.'

. . . Why hadn't anyone *told* him? The Paris flight, coming in. That was what had woken him up, that racketing roar. Jenny passing by. Overhead. So close to him at that moment, and he hadn't known.

'I wish Wendy had a bigger place. She could put me up. As it is, I'll just have to stick it out. How are *you* coping?'

Alec was right. It didn't do a blind bit of good. Nothing does.

'Remember a boy called Cantwell? On your staff?'

'Cantwell?'

'I've borrowed his room. In Cardiff.'

'Cantwell? He's dead.'

'Yes. Well, not borrowed. Sort of taken over.'

'Shot himself, didn't he? A bad business, that.'

'Yes, it was.'

'So is this a bad business. Maybe,' Corder said, 'we should both get pissed.' Clambering rather awkwardly to his feet, he opened an adjacent cupboard and took out yet another bottle of the double malt. 'Where's your glass?'

'Here.'

'Here. Right. Well, the truth of the matter *is*, he blotted his copybook. Pretty badly.'

'Who did?'

'That Cantwell fellow. We had to sack him. He'd been given notice. Of course, no one imagined that he'd go and . . . do *that*. But the fact remains.'

Get pissed. It wasn't a bad idea. 'Nobody said anything about that at the inquest.'

'Hell, no. No point in washing your dirty linen. He wasn't a special friend of yours, was he? Or a protégé? Or anything like that?'

'Not really, no. I was just a little puzzled—'

'You see, that's how it *is*. We all know there's a lot of it going on but no one wants to admit to it. Because if you do that, you imply it's been successful. And then the fat's in the fire, as the saying goes.'

Dobie had already suspected that that other whisky bottle in the sitting-room had taken a certain amount of punishment that morning. '. . . I'm sorry Alec. I don't follow you at all.'

'You really don't?'

'I really don't.'

'Well . . . Perhaps I'm getting whatchamaycallit about it. Paranoid. That's the word. Oh God,' Corder said. 'Industrial espionage, we call it. Professional misconduct. Of course when you've got the evidence you've no choice but to act on it. It's quite a serious matter. You can understand that.'

'Yes, but . . . Is that what he was doing? *Cantwell?*'

'It's what a whole lot of people are doing. All over the country. Picking up a little piece here, a little piece there. And somewhere there's a clever chappie who collects it all together and adds it all up. Of course *he* wasn't the clever chappie. Cantwell wasn't. A snippet provider, you might say. But that's bad enough.'

The aircraft had passed on now, was gaining height over the Channel. Dobie was having some difficulty in collecting his thoughts. In adding them all up. His mind was still on a small safety-belted figure, leaning forwards a little in her seat, gazing fixedly out into the hard-driving rain. 'But you make hi-fi components, don't you? Stereo speakers and so on?'

'Yes, we do. But now we're going into hearing aids. No great harm in my telling you that, the cat's been out of that little bag for some time back.' Alec's voice had gained a little in confidence and enthusiasm; he was talking shop and back on familiar ground. 'We're going into hearing aids in a very big way, in fact I've just been looking at a new production site in Birmingham. It'll be hard getting hold of the workforce I'll need down here.'

'You think that's likely to be lucrative?'

'You know what they cost, those little miniaturised ones that go inside your ear? . . . Three to five hundred they'll set you back. I plan to produce a *more* effective model that'll retail at sixty pounds and that's including VAT. Not just in the UK, either. Throughout the Common Market and in the USA. You know how many partially deaf people there are over an area that size? . . . No, nor do I. But the mind boggles, right? And all that with a guaranteed six per cent profit margin. A good investment opportunity, wouldn't you say?'

'You're going to end up pretty rich, if it all works out.'

'I'm rich already.'

'Well, yes. So you are.'

The classic one-two with the shotgun, Dobie thought. First you blast the ears off the kids with your high-voltage amplifiers, then you sell them cheap hearing aids when they've grown up. It can't fail.

'. . . But,' Corder said, a little wistfully, 'if the Min. of Health takes it up, as they're almost bound to, it'd probably get me a peerage. You know, Jane had her heart set on that. I don't know that I'm so very keen. It's not as though I had a son or someone who would . . . But there you are.' He paused for a space. 'Shit. Sometimes you wonder.'

'What kind of stuff did Cantwell have access to?'

'*I* don't know. Ask Roger Michaels about it. My security bloke. *He*'ll have all the details if you're interested. But you didn't come here to talk about my business problems, did you?'

'No. Not really.'

'Let's take another little drink to it, then.'

With all that liquid refreshment sloshing around inside him, Dobie didn't fancy getting straight back into his car and driving off. Not with the minatory figure of a hefty police constable still guarding the front gate. A little fresh air and exercise was first of all indicated. Accordingly, Dobie turned sharp left on leaving, entering thus the Pantmawr garden, and began to walk up and down on the lawn. It was an extensive lawn but very patchy, the grass clearly finding the salt sea air not much to its liking. At some fifty yards' distance from the house it indeed gave up the struggle completely, yielding to a rough sandy shingle which degenerated in turn into the shale and loose rocks that marked the edge of the sea-cliff; not a very precipitous cliff, but steep enough for a low protective wall to have been built along it. On this stone wall Dobie saw that Wendy was seated, shoulders slightly hunched, gazing out to sea. He wasn't sure that she'd be in a mood to appreciate company, but as his unwary approach had not gone unremarked he couldn't very well sheer away without at least the appearance of discourtesy. He continued his approach, therefore, and sat down beside her. Like many middle-aged men, Dobie felt a certain unease when conversing with the grown-up children of old friends; you never knew whether to include them, so to speak, within the aura of that friendship or to treat them as independent entities, and fiercely independent entities at that. He even felt a little uneasy about Wendy *qua* entity; there had always been something a bit tomboyish about her which probably had something to do with what Alec had said. A daughter instead of a son. Girls are all too often aware of these things.

Anyway, a minute or so had gone by and neither of

them had so far said anything. It was Wendy, in fact, who broke the silence first. '. . . I just can't think of anything to say.'

'No,' Dobie said, shifting his position slightly. 'There isn't anything, really.'

'It's even worse for you than it is for Dad. I mean you hadn't been married all that long, had you?'

'Not long. But I wouldn't say it makes it any worse.'

'I didn't really know her very well. I met her a few times *here*, of course, at Mum's coffee mornings and things like that. She seemed very nice. Maybe,' Wendy said, 'a little bit *young* for you.'

Dobie wondered if a certain bitchiness of disposition was an inherited quality or latent in the species. *With women, I suppose it usually is*. It might have been Jane talking. 'I didn't really know her very well, either.'

'Maybe you'd rather not talk about it.'

'I'd rather not *have* to talk about it. But with you, it's all right.'

'I know what you mean,' Wendy said. 'Yes. It's so *awful*.'

A tear rolled slowly down her left cheek. Dobie, suddenly reminded of that time with Kate in the cemetery, how many weeks ago? . . . reached for his handkerchief again. But Wendy shook her head.

'I liked her but I didn't like Mum. *That*'s what's awful. And it's no use Dad telling me not to worry about it, it's just the same with him. They didn't get on. I know it and *he* knows it but he won't admit it. Parents are just *stupid* about things like that.'

'That's what my students tell me sometimes. But quite often they're mistaken. When you're that age,' Dobie said, 'it's quite easy to mistake the nature of a relationship. I suppose at *any* age, for that matter.'

'Well, I think I know more about it than you do.'

'People *are* stupid,' Dobie said. 'I'm not denying that.'

But that's not what makes them unhappy, he thought, walking away. It should do. But it doesn't. No one worries much about being stupid. It's always other people's stupidity that worries them. And makes them feel miserable. That wasn't logical. Though in another way it was. It was logical and it was illogical. That wasn't possible. Not possible for him to start driving, either. Not like this. He'd just go on walking for a little while longer . . .

Black coffee again. The balance of polar opposites, Dobie thought. Whisky and black coffee. Logical and illogical. Jane and Jenny. Ghetto-blasters and hearing aids. No end to the series. He drank black coffee and groaned as Kate at once poured him out another steaming cupful.

'Go on. Drink the rest of it up. And then you can sleep it off. You should be dam' well ashamed of yourself but you know that already.'

'Bollocks. I'm as chirpy as a cricket. Hey, listen. Kate?'

'*Now* what?'

'About the keys.'

'What keys?'

'Keys to this place. This room. Has anyone else got them? Because someone's been *in* there, you see.'

'With designs on your virtue? . . . Wasn't me. Maybe the neighbour's cat.'

'No. I'm not joking. You always keep this room locked, don't you?'

'*And* the front door. *And* the clinic. I'm careful about that. I have to be.'

'All the same, someone took Sammy's hat and raincoat and then brought them back. With this note in the raincoat pocket.'

Kate took it and read it much as Corder had done. 'I don't get it.'

'That's the note that was on Jane Corder's door when I arrived that night. And that's the hat and raincoat the man who killed her was wearing. I wasn't going to tell you about it because I thought you might be worried . . . But . . . I do have to know about the keys.'

'Are you going to tell Jackson about it? That's more to the point.'

'No,' Dobie said. 'I'm not.'

'Because you think it isn't important?'

'Because I think it is.'

'God, Dobie, are you *sure*?'

'Am I sure of my facts? Yes. Am I sure that I know what I'm doing? No. Sammy must have had the keys. What happened to them?'

'I've got them.'

'He could have had them copied and given them to someone else.'

'Why should he have? Why should anyone want to pinch his raincoat? You say they're facts but they don't make any kind of sense.'

'They're facts for all that. Your clinic's open every morning, isn't it? And again in the evenings? Anyone could walk in and out. You wouldn't know.'

'That's why Sammy always kept his door locked when he was out at work.' Kate was looking round the room now as though she'd never seen it before. With her little button eyes bright as a bird's. Hers was a bright face, when you looked at it closely. Not very pretty, no. But bright.

'I'll tell you something else I learned this morning,' Dobie said. 'Alec told me. They gave Sammy the sack.'

'They *sacked* him? I don't believe it.'

'Alec should know.'

'What for?'

'For stealing. Or that's what it amounts to.'

'This is crazy,' Kate said. 'Stealing *what*?'

'Information. You know. Industrial spinach,' Dobie said. 'Design plans and that sort of thing. I'll try to find out a bit more about it tomorrow.'

'But that man didn't say anything about it at the inquest.'

'That's what *I* said. And Alec said they didn't want it to come out. No point in it, since Sammy was dead.'

'I can see *that*.' The eyes were now two lambent points of fire. God, Dobie thought, she *is* quite pretty when she gets angry. The Irish blood, maybe. 'They give him the sack and he shoots himself, yes, that looks kind of bad. So we won't mention it. But if the coroner bites me in the neck for knowing that he had a gun, that's my own silly fault. Too bad. If he weren't a friend of yours, *I'd* shoot the bugger.'

'That wasn't quite how he put it.'

'I'll bet it wasn't.'

'I'll find out about it, Kate. Really I will.'

'Forget it,' Kate said. 'You've got troubles of your own.'

'I *want* to find out about it.'

'Well, I *don't* want you to. I know you mean well but you're accident-prone.'

'Okay,' Dobie said. 'So you're a doctor. Why don't we go out for a little stroll together? – so you can keep a watchful eye on me.'

Kate considered this suggestion thoughtfully.

'Well . . . It *is* quite a nice evening.'

Monday morning. And business as usual, at Corder Acoustics. All the staff carrying on regardless.

In keeping with this outdated military philosophy, the desk had a plaque on it which said *MAJOR R.M. MICHAELS MC*. The desk wasn't as large as Dickie Bird's and the office wasn't nearly as imposing, its walls being festooned with papers suspended from bulldog clips and with dilapidated year planners; behind the desk, however, Major Michaels was getting the show on the road with customary zest, barking vigorously into a telephone. 'Of course, Mr Corder, if that's what you wish . . . No, no problem at all. I'll do that thing . . .' He put down the receiver and smiled at Dobie, displaying in the process an alarming number of gleamingly white incisors. 'Well, that seems to be all in order, Mr Dobie. Now then. Cantwell, I think you said . . .'

He swivelled his chair vigorously to the right and then swivelled it back again.

'. . . What can I tell you?'

'I understand you have a security problem.'

'Well, yes, we have. I have to agree. Hearing aids. Ha! *Bloody hell!* Hearing aids! You can just imagine it.'

'Well, not quite,' Dobie said diffidently. 'Not, that's to say, from your viewpoint.'

'They're so damned *small*,' Michaels said. 'Like, *tiny*. You stick one in your ear and it's almost invisible, that's how it's *supposed* to be, and of course there are other places where you could stick one, if you see what I mean, like where the monkey put the nuts, that's supposing you wanted to smuggle one out of here. No way of stopping it. Other than to make sure no unauthorised person gets hold of one in the first place.'

'And that's what you've done?'

'That's what we *try* to do. But then there's all kinds of technical griff that'd be very useful to any well-informed competitor. Design print-outs, test records, calculations, production forecasts even . . .'

'Who would want to buy that sort of stuff?'

'Well, I like to think we have the British opposition just about weighed up. We know *them* and they know *us* and no hard feelings. But there's quite a number of those Common Market chaps I don't know from a cake of soap and don't know that I want to frightfully. The Jerries are the worst, of course, but the Frogs and even some of the Swedes are getting pretty hot. It's all becoming a bit of a nightmare, frankly.'

'Yes,' Dobie said. 'I can see that it must be.'

'Specially when you're dealing with people who may be simply whizzo at hi-tech electronics but otherwise never seem to know if it's Easter Island they're on or Maundy Thursday. They just shove papers and things into their overalls and then go buzzing about from place to place like a blue-arsed bee in a bakery. Okay, so it's just plain carelessness, but what if every once in a while it isn't?'

Dobie was somewhat taken aback by the Major's style of conversation, in which the phrases came out in a series of explosions, each concluded with a formidable snap of the teeth, the general effect being that of a man proceeding with undue haste across an exceptionally well-prepared minefield. 'Was that,' he asked, 'what Sammy Cantwell did?'

With a powerful thrust of his right leg the Major spun his chair round through a hundred and eighty degrees and then spun it back again; bewilderingly thus confronted, albeit briefly, with the back of the Major's neatly-trimmed head, Dobie wondered if some weird new form of callisthenics was being practised and if so, if he should not do the same. He decided, however, against it; probably wisely. 'Just exactly that,' Michaels said. 'The boss may be prepared to shut an eye or even both if his senior staff bend the rules a little, but that doesn't go for junior staff in the Research Section. No way, José. He got the boot *and* deserved it.'

'Did he know *Mrs* Corder?'

Michaels seemed to find this question a trifle disconcerting. He revealed his inner perturbation by raising his right eyebrow about one-thousandth of an inch. 'Why do you ask that?'

'She came round here, didn't she? On occasion?'

'Yes, she did. On occasion. I once asked if I shouldn't issue her with a pass but she got quite shirty about it. So we let it ride. No – the reason why your question surprised me a little,' the Major said, adjusting the set of his sleeve to show the greater part of an unidentifiable regimental cufflink, 'one of my blokes saw her talking to him the day before he got copped. He thought it was odd because she didn't usually stop off to chat up the junior staff. No reason why she shouldn't, of course. It just wasn't something she often did.'

Certainly hob-nobbing with the *hoi polloi* had never been Jane's sort of thing. 'Did she seem to know who he was? Or was she just generally dispensing a gracious word?'

'Not knowing, can't say. The *really* odd thing was that he later denied the incident had ever taken place.'

'Really? When?'

'Very next day. When I was pointing out to him the error of his ways and handing him his cards. I mean, it was just a casual question I put to him, but he lied about it, just the way he lied about everything else. Never seen her, he said, much less spoken to her. He couldn't have known I had a witness. Two, in fact, since my lot always go around in pairs.'

'And that's the only time she's ever spoken to one of the junior staff?'

'Oh no, I don't say that. But it doesn't very often happen. Other than to say "Good morning" and so forth. Except to Wendy, of course. When she's here.'

'Wendy?'

'Don't you know Wendy? The boss's daughter?'

'*Wendy*, of course I know Wendy.' Dobie shook his head. For a moment or two, his thoughts had wandered.

'I don't think she came in today, but that's understandable. Of course,' the Major said, trying out a new exercise which involved tipping his chair over backwards until he appeared to be in imminent danger of capsize, 'the old man'd like her to go into the business on the management side. Natural enough as he doesn't have a son. But I don't believe she's really all that keen. Women in business . . .' He scrutinised the ceiling keenly, pondering the matter, before abruptly coming back to an even keel. 'It might be better if there were more of them. We just haven't got used to them yet.'

'That's a very enlightened view,' Dobie said. 'Personally, I—'

'Oh well, as employers go, old Corder's enlightened enough. The trouble is, it don't always cut both ways. I mean the ladies have got to liberalise some of their views as well and it isn't easy for them. I don't think our Wendy was one little bit chuffed when she got to hear about Sinful Susan but that's the sort of thing I mean. A son, now, would understand at once. You can't expect a *daughter* to.'

'Ah,' Dobie said, out of his depth but struggling manfully.

'That's another aspect of the problem, of course. The security problem. You just can't stop people gossiping, not even about the boss. *Especially* not about the boss. Men are *worse* than women, believe you me.'

'I suppose you've had her checked? Security-wise?'

This was Dobie at his most brilliantly guileful.

'Susan? Oh Lord, yes. She's perfectly okay. Nice quiet young lady. Husband's in insurance, I believe. Of course *she* never comes round the office. Naturally not.'

'Susan . . . I've forgotten her other name . . .'

'Not a frightful lot of people know that. The old man likes to keep it pretty much under his hat. It's Strange.'

'Well, not altogether. In the circumstances.'

'Eh? . . . No, I mean her *name* is Strange.'

'Oh, I *see*. What is it?'

A faint grinding noise emerged from the Major's mouth. 'Strange is her name, for Chrissake, it's *Mrs* Strange, *Susan* Strange. I do hope I'm getting through.'

Brilliant guilefulness was not, in fact, Dobie's forte.

It was str— It was very odd how often he had this effect upon people. 'Yes, oh yes, I'm sorry, it's just that it's some time since I heard . . . I mean it has to have been going on for some little time now. Hasn't it?'

The Major's jawbones relaxed perceptibly. 'About a year or so, I would say. But what I'm really *getting* at, you can see the daughter's point of view in these cases. What she doesn't realise is that it could've been so much worse. You know, the directors of some of the companies I've worked for . . . Well, you wouldn't believe it if I were to tell you.'

'But of course, you have to keep all that side of things pretty confidential.'

'Haw haw yes,' the Major said. 'I should rather say so.'

'At least I found out what Alec's security problem is.'

'Oh? What's that?'

'The security officer.'

'It seems to be true about Sammy, though.'

'Yes.'

'So let's leave it alone.'

'It's where the connection is, though.'

'What connection?'

'Between everyone, just about. Me and Jenny and Jane and Alec and Sammy. And now this additional complication.'

'Sinful Susan?'

'Yes.'

'Is that what she is?'

'Sinful? Or a complication?'

'Skip it. You weren't all *that* surprised, were you?'

'I was in a way. I didn't know Alec had a mistress.'

'God, Dobie, people don't *say* that any more.'

'. . . Was having a bit on the side.'

'That's much better.'

'I don't see why, but never mind.'

'I'll tell you why,' Kate said. 'When my father started out in practice, he was what used to be called a family doctor. If you were on his panel you had everyone else along with you – aunts, cousins, grandparents, the lot. But then things changed and it just meant parents and children. By the time *I* was a student you could forget about the children unless you wanted to be some kind of children's specialist. And now there aren't any married couples, either. Only males and females. In other words, when they come to see me there's only me me *me*. This is a me-me-*me* society, Dobie, and I'm a me-me-*me* doctor, family doctors have gone with the dinosaurs and so have kindly fathers and loving wives and all that caboodle. *That*'s why no one says "mistress" any more. Except for a few befuddled refugees from Barchester Towers. You got to get *with* it, Dobie baby, else you're way out in Cloudsville. I'm sorry but *someone* has to let you in on the facts of life.'

'Don't be angry, Kate.'

'You're such a *cluck*.'

'I know I irritate people.'

'So did Jesus Christ. It's not *that*. Or maybe it is. You remind them of the days when things were different. You're so fucking *quaint*.'

Dobie hadn't anticipated this attack but his years of experience as a college lecturer had given him a certain expertise in the arts of ducking and weaving. 'Yes, but in those days women didn't have much say in the matter, did they? What you're talking about, it goes with being independent and having a career and so on. You can't have it—'

'Oh, shut *up*, Dobie. And stop dithering about.'

Dobie in fact wasn't dithering about but merely arranging the cassette tapes on the shelf into some semblance of order. Of course, it all depended on how you looked at it. Were he to continue the argument, the calm perseverance with which he marshalled the relevant facts would no doubt be immediately characterised as pig-headed obstinacy. It was no good saying she couldn't have it both ways when she so very obviously could.

'Just because you're married,' Kate said, 'doesn't mean you're not on your own. You can run a big business and still feel lonely. It's no one's fault. That's how the system works.'

'You said once that Sammy felt lonely.'

'So he did. But it didn't worry him. *He* knew all about the system.'

'He must have had old-fashioned tastes, though.'

'Why do you say that?'

'Well, look at *this*.' Dobie held up a cassette box. 'Cole Porter. That's before *my* time, even.'

'Isn't Mozart? Don't you *like* Cole Porter?'

'That's not the point. I don't listen to much pop music. Of course Jenny used to . . .'

He stopped, staring miserably down at the tape in his hand. Argument ended. Kate watched him in silence for some little while, then slid an arm round his waist and squeezed it gently. '. . . Hello, sailor.'

'Hello,' Dobie said.

'I'm sorry. That all came out a bit differently to the way I meant.'

'It's not that,' Dobie said. 'It isn't anything you *said*. Do you mind if I play this?'

'Play that tape? . . . Why should *I* mind? Be my guest.'

She sat down a little heavily at the work-desk as Dobie turned towards the cassette-player, pressing the power and the ejection switches. There was, as he then saw, a tape in the machine already. He pushed the ejection cover closed again and pressed the play button. Nothing happened.

'What's the matter? Can't you work it?'

'Wait a moment,' Dobie said. 'There seems to be a temporary hitch . . .'

He tried the rewind button. The spools whizzed obediently round for several seconds, then stopped with a click. He tried again.

'. . . *Hey Kate*,' Sammy Cantwell said. '*This is Sammy*.'

Kate's normally pale face had gone considerably paler than usual.

'You scared the shit out of me, you know that?'

'I didn't mean to,' Dobie said. 'I'd no idea . . .'

'I should have . . . Why did I never *think* of it?'

'The police must have missed out on it, too.'

'Yes, but Sammy always sent me messages that way. He never wrote letters. *They* didn't know that. But *I* did.'

'What sort of messages?'

'Anything at all. Like he needed some groceries or maybe he'd be working late, he did that sometimes . . . If he couldn't catch me because I was in the clinic or out somewhere, he'd pop a tape in through my letterbox. I just didn't *think* about it, that's what bugs me.'

'But he *didn't* put it through your letterbox.'

'No. That's the point.'

'Because he didn't have time.'

'Is that what you think?'

'It looks that way,' Dobie said.

'Let's hear it again . . .'

Dobie set the tape in motion once more.

'Hey Kate . . . This is Sammy, look . . . I haven't seen you since yesterday and what happened was, they gone and given me the sack or anyway told me not to come back, there was an unpleasantness, y'know? . . . So what I'm going to do, I'm going up to town to talk things over with my uncle but I'll be back Monday and what I'll do, I'll leave part of the rent money on the table, okay? . . . Right now I got someone coming round I've been sort of helping out and maybe we can get it fixed up so I'll get some more bread, one good turn deserves another sort of thing, only I'm not too sure how it'll go because it's all got a bit complicated and I won't be able to help out any more because of something else that happened at bloody Corders . . . Look, I only mention it because any old way I should be getting a few more bucks so I'll be paying you the rest of my back rent soon as I get back from London, okay? . . . Okay. See you then . . .'

Dobie reached over and checked the tape again. 'He must have recorded that the day he died, since he says he got sacked the day before . . .'

'And he was expecting someone round . . .'

'So he must have made that tape just before whoever it was arrived . . . but he didn't put it in your letterbox or even take it out of the machine because . . .'

'He was dead,' Kate said.

A contemplative silence.

'Can you make sense of it any other way?'

'No,' Kate said. 'I can't.'

'Nor can I.'

'So we'd better call Jackson.'

'Yes,' Dobie said. 'I think so.'

That night Jackson had got in some kip at last and he was, in consequence, feeling a good deal more chipper today. But the pile of papers on his tray was higher than ever. Foxy Boxy had moved into his office to help him deal with them, but even their joint efforts barely served to stem the tide. And the telephone kept ringing, which didn't help. Every cloud, however, had a silver lining. Pontin wasn't in the office today. *That* helped.

And as the sheaves of paper were quietly disposed of, now and again a snippet of useful information came through. 'Seen the B42 from the forensic lab?'

Jackson grunted. 'What's it say?'

'Says there's nothing wrong with that whisky.'

'What whisky?'

'The whisky that Dobie character says he drank. We got his prints on the tumbler and that cut-glass thing—'

'Decanter.'

'Whatever. But the booze was okay. So his story's a load of cobblers. But then,' Box said, 'we always thought so.' He pushed the report across the desk. Jackson didn't pick it up but rubbed his forehead instead.

'It got him his alibi, though. Don't forget that.'

'You'd have thought he could have come up with something a little less . . .'

'Improbable.'

'Barmy, I was going to say.'

'I haven't seen my wife and kids,' Jackson said, 'these past three days. Nor have you, hardly. What does that make *us*?'

'There have to be easier ways, it's true.'

'Makes you want to turn to crime,' Jackson said. The telephone rang and he answered it. 'Jackson, yes . . . Who? . . . Oh *no* . . . I mean yes, Mr Dobie. We were just talking about *you* . . .'

Back in Sammy's room Kate and Dobie looked at each other.

'How long?'

'He said about twenty minutes.'

Kate nodded and Dobie sat down wearily on the foot of the bed. Over by the far wall the tape was turning smoothly, soothingly, not Sammy this time but

Oscar Petersen, fingers expertly gliding over piano keys, pulling a simple theme this way and that, worrying it like a terrier. Behind the piano, Barney Kessel's guitar. And behind the guitar an unheard voice, singing on the cracks between the notes, tumty-*tum* tummy-*tum*-ti-tum. 'This was one of them,' Dobie said.

'One of what?'

'One of the songs that Jenny was always singing. "One of Those Things", it's called. She didn't know the words, of course. Nor do I.' The track coming to an end in a triumphant ascending ripple, Dobie's head cocked a little to one side, listening. 'It's funny. I've got quite a good ear for a tune. Most mathematicians have, or so I'm told. But I can never . . . Mind you, it's catchy, isn't it? Sticks in the mind.'

'A lot of people have thought so. What the hell are you *on* about, Dobie?'

Oscar started off on another track and Dobie nodded.

'Yes. "Night And Day". That one, too. Talking about mathematics, did you know that the statistical laws of probability relate to coincidence? Using the word, that is, in its technical sense. Which I suppose isn't really—'

Kate got to her feet. 'I think I'll go downstairs. Catch the doorbell when it rings. I've suddenly started liking this room a whole lot less than ever.'

Dobie didn't reply, or even look up until the door had closed behind her. He wondered, after she'd gone, why she had said that. He was beginning to like this room very much. It was the right size and the right shape to comfort an inner loneliness. It was a good room for reading or for listening to music or for spending long hours stooped over a monitor screen, except that the hours wouldn't be long because time didn't seem to have too much meaning here. Maybe Sammy had found that out. It was very likely.

It conformed, in other words, to the statistical laws of probability. From whence you derived the concept of the possible. And hence the idea of certain concrete possibilities. Dobie got up, too, and began to search.

Under the bed, first of all. Not only peering into the shadows there, but probing with his fingertips. He didn't find anything. The chest of drawers didn't reveal anything very extraordinary, either; nor did the shelves where the cassette-player stood and where Oscar now played "In the Still of the Night", slow melancholy chords breaking up abruptly into agitated waves like those on the surface of a wind-ruffled sea, though Dobie took down the books that also stood there one by one and leafed through them carefully. The wardrobe . . . Dobie opened the wardrobe. Sammy's suits and sports coats and his famous raincoat all hanging in a row, Dobie's own spare suit alongside. On the top shelf the hat, a baseball cap, a dozen or so pairs of socks. On the bottom shelf . . . a bit of a mess. Three pairs of shoes and a pair of trainers, these last thrown in indiscriminately. A small pile of six or eight soft-porn magazines and a bigger collection of *New Scientist* weeklies. A peculiar tangle of wires and pulleys that turned out to be a discarded chest-expander. A cardboard box containing a computerised chess set. A plastic bag, bearing a familiar logo, containing moderately heavy objects that clinked. Dobie took it out, opened it. Inside were two one-pound jars of peanut butter.

Jackson made a neat polyurethane packet of Sammy and then slid him carefully into a large brown evidence envelope. '. . . Egg on my face all right,' he said. '*And* all down the front of my best suit. How we missed out on that, I'll never know.'

'It's his voice all right,' Kate said. Now that she had calmed down a little, her former mood of aggressiveness seemed to have returned. 'I can swear to it if you want. You can screw around all you want with voiceprints but you'll be wasting your time. That's Sammy.'

'No need for anyone to swear to anything,' Jackson said placatorily. 'Though tomorrow I'll be asking you for a statement as to how exactly you came to find it. A formal statement, that is. And then I'll have to try and make sure the Superintendent doesn't get to see it.' He made a soft clucking noise with his tongue, expressive of incredulity and regret. 'You know, if you happen across a bloke on the floor with his brains blown out and a gun in his hand you tend not to look too far beyond the obvious. Maybe in books you do. In police work you don't. I'll admit I really intended to come back here and take a bit more of a dekko, but I was having a busy day and somehow . . . Well, they can skin me alive on this one and they probably will, if that's any consolation to you.'

'You agree it would have made a difference? To the verdict?'

'Of course it would, Mr Dobie. The case'll have to be reopened. I don't say that tape makes suicide a complete impossibility, he could have had a sudden change of mind or . . . But it shifts the odds in favour of murder, instead of the other way round. And if so, somebody fooled us. Fooled us completely. And we don't like that.'

'Only because you didn't have all the evidence.'

'Because we didn't *find* all the evidence. That could have been a worse mistake than you probably think.'

'In what way?'

'Well, I'll tell you. What worries me is that someone may have thought it too damned *easy*. Setting it up so we'd swallow it hook, line and sinker, as the saying has it.'

'And felt encouraged to do it again?'

'That's *it*, Mr Dobie. That's how it happens. It's like going over the top of a hill, for some people. All of a sudden there's nothing to stop you.'

Jackson's remark may not have been intended to provoke a sudden heavy silence, but it did. After a while

Dobie started to scratch his kneecap, his fingernails making a rasping noise against the cloth of his trouser-leg like heavy breathing. 'Are you saying you can see some kind of connection . . . ?'

'Perhaps we shouldn't draw *that* conclusion. Not just yet.'

'Perhaps we shouldn't.' But Kate, who was getting used to Dobie's little ways, sensed that he had now come to *some* kind of a conclusion or, anyway, decision. 'I suppose,' he said, staring moodily at his recently-relinquished knee-joint, 'you checked the room for fingerprints? When it happened?'

'We did,' Jackson said. 'But maybe not thoroughly enough. Don't worry on that account, though. Nine o'clock tomorrow morning I'll have the dabs boys round and this time they won't miss out a thing, I promise you that.'

'Can they still *get* prints? I mean, it's been over a week . . .'

'Oh Lord, yes. On any kind of a decent surface—'

'Glass?'

'What?'

'Is glass any good?'

Dobie had of course to be joking, or so Jackson's expression suggested. 'Glass? That's just about the best.'

'That's what I thought.' Dobie picked up the plastic bag from the floor at his feet. 'You may like to check on those for a start.'

Jackson opened the bag and peered suspiciously into it. 'Where'd these come from?'

'Bottom shelf of the wardrobe. Could you check on them tonight? As a personal favour?'

'What makes you think I owe you any personal favours?'

'I think you owe Sammy Cantwell one.'

Jackson nodded slowly. 'I might do at that. Just what

is it that you're holding back on *this* time, Mr Dobie?'

'I'm not holding back on anything,' Dobie said. 'Detective-Sergeant Box knows all about it.'

'All about what? Peanut butter?'

'Yes,' Dobie said. 'Peanut butter.'

All kinds of nice breakfast things were on Kate's kitchen table. Corn flakes, toast on a toast rack, unsalted butter, Oxford marmalade, sugar in a bowl, milk in a jug, hot coffee in a pot and on two plates the dissected remnants of two large Scotch kippers. The one notable omission was remedied by Inspector Jackson who, arriving towards the end of the meal, plonked the two unopened jars heftily down on the table. This, prior to turning round a kitchen chair and sitting down on it back to front. The Major, Dobie thought, hadn't tried out that one.

'The prints on those damned jars of yours,' Jackson said without preamble, 'are whose I haven't much doubt but that you thought they were, Mr Dobie. So what I want to know is, what's the game? Is it a private fight or can anyone join in?'

'Have some coffee, Inspector.' Kate was in a sunnier mood this morning.

'I won't, thank you. I'd prefer an answer to my question.'

Not so Jackson.

'I'm not playing any kind of game,' Dobie said a little indistinctly, his mouth being more than half full of buttered toast. 'I just wanted to be sure about it. The peanut butter by itself would hardly have convinced you, any more than this jar of marmalade would. It's very nice, by the way. I can recommend it.'

'Now look,' Jackson said. 'The Chief Constable has reopened the Cantwell file all right, so in effect I'm now undertaking a murder inquiry. *Another* murder inquiry, as if I didn't have enough under my belt already. I'd be obliged if you'd both treat this as a serious matter.'

'I can only tell you what I think,' Dobie said, reaching across the table for another slice. He was breakfasting more energetically than usual; perhaps his change of ambience was conducive to a hearty appetite.

'That might do for a start.'

'Well, *if* it was murder, someone took the trouble to make it look like a suicide.'

'That would seem to be the case, yes.'

'And that *someone* was probably the person Sammy was waiting to see when he recorded that message for Kate.'

'Since that person has never come forward, I agree that's quite likely.'

'Who was also very probably the person Sammy used to lend his room to, on occasion. That was how he was *helping out*, as he put it. Doing somebody a good turn, he said. That's what I think he must have meant.'

Jackson had turned his head to stare at Kate. 'What's he mean, *lend his room*? You never told me anything about that, doctor.'

'Because he never told *me*. I didn't know.' Kate, in turn, was staring towards Dobie. 'This is the first I've heard about it.'

'Either he lent his keys to someone who had them copied, or he had them copied himself. Someone else has the keys – that's the important point. So as to use the room when he wasn't there. Which is of course how someone else found out where he kept the gun.'

'Why,' Jackson asked, 'would anyone want to borrow his room?'

'Because being a bed-sitter, it's got a bed in it. Quite a comfortable one, in fact.'

Jackson stared uncomfortably at what he had written in his notebook, and chewed the end of his pencil. *Borrowed* or *burrowed*? . . . Bit of a puzzler, that one.

'You mean it was used for purposes of sexual assignation?'

'Yes.'

'Ah,' Jackson said.

For purposes of sexual assassination, he wrote.

After a while, he asked, 'Why?'

'It's a universal human urge. Or so they tell me.'

'No, I mean . . . why *that* room? It's not what I'd call a very syphilitic apartment.'

'I think *sybaritic* is the word you want.'

'Well, is it?'

'No. But it's convenient. Or the location is. With a doctor's clinic right beneath and with the same entrance door.'

'Aha. So I had the right word after all.'

'You miss the point,' Dobie said testily. 'It's convenient because you've got people going in and out of that door all day, or at least from ten to twelve-thirty and from five till seven. And you've even got a reasonable excuse if by ill luck you should bump into somebody you know. You picked up this nasty cough from somewhere—'

'Did your wife have a nasty cough, Mr Dobie? . . . Because those are her prints on the peanut butter jars, as I'm sure you know very well.'

A rather unmannerly interruption, Dobie thought, but he took it none the less in his stride. 'I don't think she really meant to leave them here. She just put them away and forgot about them.'

'But what was she *doing* here?'

'I thought I explained all that. She was, er . . . having a little bit on the side. I'm told that's the phrase that's currently in vogue.'

'But—'

'You've seen our flat. It wouldn't have done at all for that sort of thing, not on any kind of a regular basis. What with all those other flats around us and people always peering out through the windows. Same would apply to a hotel, anywhere in Cardiff. Besides,' Dobie said, considering a further interesting possibility, 'she might have quite *liked* that room. I know I do. It's so different to the flat, you see. So warm and dark. And sordid. You often get that with rather finicky girls, don't you think? . . . A sort of *nostalgie de la boue*? . . .'

'Oh indeed,' Jackson said. He started to write in his notebook *Noss* and then crossed it out. 'A back-to-the-womb complex, as like as not.' He then chewed the end of his pencil some more, gazing meditatively at Dobie the while. 'Is that all you've got to say on the matter, Mr Dobie?'

'Well—'

'Or are you going on to tell me your wife killed Mr Cantwell?'

'I can't say for certain that she didn't. But I'm reasonably confident she didn't kill Jane Corder and then hit herself on the back of the head. I doubt very much if she even *knew* Sammy. But of course it takes two people to make an assignation. I don't think *she* was the one Sammy was helping out – as he puts it. Or the one he was expecting to see the morning he died.'

'So who was it?'

'I don't know.'

'You've no idea at all?'

'None at all. At one time I thought I had, but I was wrong.'

'You were wrong but you still had some reason to suppose . . . ?'

'Some reason, yes. But nothing definite.'

'Did you *do* anything about it?'

'Such as what?'

'*Duw*, I don't know. Any of the things you'd *expect* a husband to do . . . Ask her about it? Smack her on the hooter? Even *try* and find out who it was she was seeing?'

'No,' Dobie said. 'I didn't do anything like that.'

'And you didn't say anything about it to *us*. When you made your statement.'

'No,' Dobie said. 'I didn't have any facts. Besides, it would have been . . . embarrassing.'

'*Embarrassing?* . . . Yes, I can see *that*.'

'I suppose at the time I thought it would all blow over pretty quickly,' Dobie said. 'Or if it didn't, that'd be all right, too, because things weren't going all that well between us anyway. In any case—'

'In any case the boy friend wasn't who you thought it was.'

'No. It wasn't.'

'So maybe you'd best leave all that side of things to the police.'

'Is that what most people do in these cases? I wouldn't have thought—'

'I didn't mean *that*, exactly.' Jackson in fact wasn't at all sure what he *had* meant and decided that that particular issue need be argued no further. What he chiefly wanted to do now was go away and wrap his brains for a while in embrocation-soaked cotton wool; the trouble with Dobie was that, whatever it was he had, it seemed to be catching. '. . . Well, the boys may be working in the other room for a little while longer but if it's all the same to you I'll be off. It looks like being another busy day.'

'And,' Dobie said, 'if you *should* chance to find any prints there whose presence you can't account for—'

'Confidential information, that is,' Jackson said severely. 'You've stuck your oar in quite far enough, Mr Dobie. From now on, leave everything to us.'

After he had gone Kate began to collect the breakfast things and pile them in the sink, making, Dobie thought, an unnecessary clatter in the process. He stationed himself in his customary washing-up position and was about to twiddle the hot water tap when Kate pushed his hand away. 'No, don't do that. I'll manage.'

Dobie knew what the matter was and felt contrite. '. . . I sprang it on you, Kate, didn't I? I really am sorry.'

'Yes, you damn well *did*.'

'But I couldn't say anything to you until I was sure. How could I?'

She withdrew her hand, seemingly slightly mollified by this apology. 'He may have given you good advice at that.'

'You think so?'

'You know what you've just *done*, don't you? . . . You've given him the one thing he didn't have before. A motive.'

Dobie didn't get it. 'What, for killing Sammy?'

'*No*, you berk. For killing Jenny.'

'What, just because . . . ? I wouldn't have done that. Even if I'd known for sure, and I made it quite clear to him I didn't.'

'People don't always need to know for sure.' She grabbed a coffee-cup as it hurtled from Dobie's clutching fingers towards the floor. 'Look, thanks very much. But you dry.'

'It might be wise. I do seem to manage a rather high breakage rate.' Dobie changed places with her, temporarily assuming command of the dishcloth. 'I do need to know for sure. Knowing for sure is my métier, so to speak. Or let's say establishing parabolas of reasonable certainty.'

'It's just as well you didn't tell Jackson that. It hurt a lot, didn't it? It must have.'

'You mean Jenny's being unfaithful? Oh well, I'm sure people don't use that expression any more, either.'

'Perhaps they don't. But that doesn't affect the way they feel about it. What I really meant, though, was *telling* him about it. After all . . . you didn't have to.'

'I did,' Dobie said. 'That's the thing about syllogistic chains.' He stooped to retrieve the shattered remnants of a saucer from the floor. 'They're so beautiful you just can't keep it to yourself if you hit upon one. You could almost call it a crime. Sorry about that, it was sort of *soapy*.'

'That was the natural result of its having been immersed in detergent liquid. Look, Dobie, why don't you sit down and let the plates get nice and dry all by themselves? And what's a sillo what-you-said? I forgot to swallow my after-breakfast dictionary this morning.'

Dobie accepted this demotion resignedly and sat down once again at the kitchen table. 'It's a way of explaining something that's happened when the odds against it happening seem to be astronomical. Like those jars of peanut butter in the wardrobe. If you or Jackson or anyone else had found them there, they wouldn't have meant anything at all. In fact they were found by maybe the only person in the world who might realise their significance, so to speak. And yet the sequence is perfectly syllogistic, once you follow the pattern. It could hardly have happened any other way.'

Kate sloshed hot water around the inside of a frying-pan. 'I still don't understand. *What* pattern?'

'Simple cause and effect. If Sammy hadn't lent his room to someone, he wouldn't have been killed. If he hadn't been killed, I wouldn't have gone to the inquest. If I hadn't gone to the inquest, I wouldn't have met you. If I hadn't met you, you wouldn't have brought me here when I was in a bit of a jam. If you hadn't brought me here, I wouldn't have found the peanut butter. It all links up.'

'Like that for-want-of-a-nail thing.'

'Exactly.'

Kate stacked the frying-pan on the dripboard and

began to wipe her hands. 'It's certainly what Sherlock Holmes would have called a singular train of events.'

'Who? . . . Oh, Sherlock *Holmes* . . .' Dobie's forehead unfurrowed in recollection. 'I don't think I've read those stories since I was at school. How does it go? *You know my methods, Watson*?'

'That's it. Not that yours are even remotely similar.'

'They are in a way. Syllogistic chains go on for ever and ever. *They* don't change according to social fads and fancies. You can work them out forwards, backwards, sideways. The problem is establishing a few links to work from in the first place, but once you've done that you should be able to find the provenance of any other event on the same chain if you go on long enough. Any event or any agent. Like who it was Sammy lent his room to.'

'You know,' Kate said, 'I think I can add just one little silly wotsit.'

'What's that?'

'Jane Corder. You know, when I saw her in the autopsy room I was sure I'd seen her before but I couldn't remember where?' She moved across to the kitchen window, looked fixedly out of it. 'I remember now. *She* was here, too.'

'*Here?*'

'Outside. Down in the street. I saw her there once. I was looking down . . . No, I wasn't. I was downstairs, in the clinic. Looking out the window. That's how it was.'

'What was she doing?'

'Nothing. Just standing there. Looking back towards me. I thought she might have been waiting for somebody, for one of the patients. It would have been about a fortnight ago.'

Dobie rubbed his chin. 'A three-pipe problem, I would say.'

'An evening session. Round about half-past six.'

'. . . Unless she was doing exactly that.'

'Waiting for one of the patients?'

'Yes.'

'She could have been.'

'Yes. It's a nice little chain,' Dobie said, 'but there's a link missing somewhere. I'll have to find it.'

In any case, it was a beautiful morning. The lark was on the wing, the snail was on the thorn, the fingerprint team was busily at work and only Detective-Inspector Jackson was notably pissed off, though possibly even he was feeling better now. Dobie drove down the long chasms of the Cardiff side streets, their murky depths illuminated by brilliant patches of sunlight, and finally emerged into the full glare of the open spaces round Roath Park. Pentycoed Road ran the length of the rise to the east of the lake and it was still a beautiful morning when Dobie got there.

Parking his trusty Fiesta at the top of the rise, he was able for a minute or two to enjoy an almost uninterrupted view of the lake's bland and unrippled surface and of the dark leaf-foliage mirrored upon it before transferring his attention to no. 51 Pentycoed Road, which also presented to his gaze a bland and unruffled surface; neat red-tiled roof, cream-colour stipple plaster, bow windows with heavy velvet curtains and all those other trappings of earnest respectability that proclaim a site to be a suitable location for a spot of mildly stimulating middle-class adultery. If the Stranges weren't prominent members of the local key club they had, Dobie decided, no business to be living in a place like that. He left his car parked on the opposite side of the street to indicate a proper respect for established custom and marched through the white-painted wrought-iron gate and up the crazy paving to the front door, feeling, though certainly not looking, like Philip Marlowe calling on General Sternwood. Confronted with a bellpush which said, archly but almost inevitably, PUSH ME, he pushed it. After an interval, brief but long enough to be suggestive of the hurried adjustment of bedspreads and wraparound peignoirs, Mrs Strange duly appeared, clad, however, in knitted skirt and an unseasonably thick woolly jumper. 'Oh,' she said, apparently by way of greeting.

'Mrs Strange? My name's Dobie.'

'You're the one who rang?'

'I'm the one who rang, yes, that does put it in a nutshell.'

'I'd expected an older person. You'd better come in.'

Dobie, on the other hand, had expected a younger. Mrs Strange was of agreeable aspect enough but certainly on the wrong (from the male viewpoint) side of thirty. She had, nevertheless, very blue eyes and very fluffy blonde hair and moved around the place in a *bouncy* sort of way. The movements in question mainly involved steering Dobie into a very, very low armchair as a sheep-dog might expertly have penned a recalcitrant sheep and then backing away from him nervously, as if confounded by this unexpected success. '. . . So you're a friend of Alec's?'

'Yes.'

'Then perhaps you'll appreciate his double malt. Or would you prefer tea? Or coffee?'

'Perhaps a *very* short whisky . . .'

'Then I think I'll join you,' Mrs Strange said. 'Just this once.'

Neither of them were particularly short ones, Dobie noted. Churlish to refuse, though. Or even to object. That business with the whisky had always been easy to explain. Alec had loads of the stuff lying around. Wash out the decanter and the glass, slosh in a refill, and all the while Dobie's peacefully asleep. Eh? . . . Wake *up*, Mr Dobie. 'This is very nice,' he said. 'I must come here more often.'

'Why not? I don't get to meet Alec's friends. Not as a rule.'

She sat down facing Dobie and crossed her legs. Even in his newly-bereaved state Dobie could not help but observe that these appendages were long and shapely. A tall girl, almost as tall as Jane. Alec being of somewhat Napoleonic build, kneehigh in other words to a bumble-bee, his tastes perhaps ran in that direction. Of course, Alec . . . It would be better, Dobie thought, to come clean and let it all hang out, if that was the proper expression.

'Alec doesn't know I've come to see you. In fact, if I were you I shouldn't want to talk to me at all. I ought to make that quite clear now because it probably won't seem quite so clear when I've finished drinking this whisky. Cheers.'

'I must say I like a man who goes so far out of his way to set my mind at rest. Why shouldn't I want to talk to you?'

'Oh, I'm not a journalist,' Dobie said hurriedly. 'Or anything like that.'

'No, you're a professor of mathematics and that's exactly what you look like.'

Dobie was only briefly taken aback by the accuracy of this apparent act of clairvoyance. 'Ah. I see. You called Alec.'

'Of course. *And* my husband. And they both said it would be quite okay so they don't seem to share your misgivings.'

'You phoned your *husband*?'

'Oh yes, I've got one of those. He's in Swansea right now on business, but I caught him at his hotel. Of course *he*'d never heard of you. But Alec had.'

'And what did Alec say?'

'Well, he seemed a bit confused at first. But he told me who you were and so on. I gather that some people think you killed your wife but *he* doesn't think you did and of course somebody killed Jane, too, and it's all very complicated and awful and there's lots about it in the newspapers and you're both having a bad time and I'm sorry. I don't know what I can do to help, but I'll try.'

'Did you *know* Jane?'

'Oh no. We never met.'

'I suppose not.' Dobie shook his head. 'Right now *I'm* a bit confused, too, because I thought I'd have to do a lot of explaining about things it seems you know about already, if you follow my drift. And then again . . . you said you phoned your husband . . . Does that mean he *knows* about Alec?'

'Of course he does. He's always known. What I don't understand is how *you* come to know about it, Mr Dobie, because Alec says he didn't tell you. I know it's silly, but he has got this thing about keeping our relationship a secret . . . And in fact it's not so silly because he has his reasons.'

'Jane would have been one of them, no doubt.'

'The chief one.'

'But now she's dead.'

'Which is probably why he said it would be all right for me to talk to you. It doesn't matter any more. Or anyway, not so much. I think it's all been getting on top of him lately, he's been working so hard . . . And now all *this*. I'd really like to help him, if I can.'

'He's never had much time to spare, ever since I've known him,' Dobie said.

'But he used to manage a couple of evenings a week when he'd finished work. Not any more. He's hardly been round to see me at all this past month. And that's a pity because it relaxes him so much. Or so he says.' Dobie could well believe it. 'I was getting quite worried about him. Max was, too.'

'Max?'

'Max, my husband. He's in insurance.'

Dobie had expected the Strange household to reveal something pretty outré in the way of life-styles but the de Maupassantish element in all this was leaving him decidedly bemused. He could detect no reflection of it in the accoutrements of the living-room where he sat, which, apart from a preponderance of potted plants and a John Bratby roofscape over the mantelpiece, seemed to be determinedly contemporary-provincial. 'How long has Alec, er . . . been coming to see you?'

'Ever since we came to Cardiff. About a year ago. We'd always lived in Leeds before, you see. That's where Max's head office is.'

'Ah,' Dobie said. 'Well, I'm afraid they know all about it in *Alec*'s office. The security man there ran a check on you, all in the ordinary line of business as I suppose. And that's how *I* got to hear of it. Apparently there's been a certain amount of, well . . . Gossip.'

'Gossip?'

'Or let's say speculation. About Alec's having a lady friend somewhere.'

'*Lady friend?*'

Probably, Dobie thought, that term wasn't in current usage, either. A series of (surely) unpalatable alternatives chased through his brain. '. . . Or whatever the current expression is.'

'Oh my God,' Mrs Strange said.

'You see they've been having some security problems—'

'Is *that* what they think?'

To his further surprise and partial consternation, she emitted a sudden little scream of bubbling laughter. '. . . Well, it serves him right, it serves him bloody well *right*. I always told him that if he wasn't careful . . .' She went into another and even more prolonged fit of the giggles. Then, as though becoming aware of the perplexed opacity of Dobie's gaze, 'Oh, I'm sorry. But it's not like that at all. I'm not Alec's lady friend. I'm a youthful indiscretion.'

'A what?'

'I'm his *daughter*, for heaven's sake.'

This idea Dobie could at once dismiss as preposterous. 'Daughter? . . . You can't be. He's got one. I know her. He hasn't got a . . . *Daughter?* Impossible. He'd know about it. Or rather *I* would. Or *someone* would. It's ridiculous.'

'*We* know about it,' Mrs Strange said, restraining her hilarity with some difficulty. 'Alec and I and Max. Yes, Wendy's his *legal* daughter and I'm sure she's a very sweet girl, she certainly seems to be. But I'm much older than she is, as you can see, and I'm not the least bit legal. Or I am in the sense that I've got some legal parents of my own and very nice ones, too. But Alec is my *real* dad. Biologically speaking.'

Dobie swallowed the remainder of his whisky very quickly. 'Yes, I see. Or I think I do. I've made a fool of myself again, but I'm getting used to that. I'm very sorry.'

'That's all right. It's not really your fault. I should feel quite flattered, in a way.' Dobie, covertly re-examining her facial features, couldn't detect the slightest resemblance to those of Alec; certainly the relationship wasn't one that could have readily been guessed at. 'I mean, Alec is still . . . Wouldn't you say? I can see why poor old Mum should have got swept off her feet, as the saying goes, especially bearing in mind he'd have been thirty years younger or thereabouts. And so would she, of course. Now that I know him quite well, I'm sure he really was in love with her. It could be I remind him of her, though he's never actually said so. Mum and I do look very much alike.'

'In that case his little peccadillo becomes much more easily understandable.'

'Now I *am* flattered. Anyone can make a mistake,' Mrs Strange said, 'but a little old-world gallantry is always greatly refreshing.'

'In my distant youth I got involved in something rather similar myself. Though as far as I know without any such altogether admirable results.'

'Actually if you knew my other dad you'd think it even more easily understandable because while he has a gentle nature he's unquestionably one of the world's most excruciating bores. *Guinness-Book-of-Records* standards. But *he* doesn't know about Alec, you see, and Mum thinks it important that he shouldn't and so do I and that's why all this hole-and-corner stuff. Apart from whatever Jane might . . . You do have to think about other people's feelings, after all.'

'What about Wendy?'

'Oh Wendy, yes, I suppose Alec thought *she* ought to know about it. We're half-sisters, after all. He brought her round here once but she didn't come again. A bit awkward for her, I expect, divided loyalty sort of thing, though Alec says she didn't get on with her mother particularly well. Of course all I know about Jane I know through Alec, so to speak. How did *you* see her? I mean *really*?'

'Well . . .' Dobie wasn't very good at executing succinct verbal portraits of his acquaintances and knew it. 'I always thought of them as being quite a well-matched couple. She was the sort of wife I imagine a very successful businessman would want to have. She *could* be very agreeable. To people she liked.'

'What about people she didn't? Was she such a *very* jealous person?'

'I suppose she was.' Dobie thought about it for a spell. '. . . Possessive, anyway. I mean, she seemed to like Jenny very much and though I'd known her for years and years myself, in no time at all she was obviously thinking of me as Jenny's husband and as such, a bit of a nuisance. But then I always thought most women were a bit that way.'

'Perhaps we do tend to be,' Mrs Strange said. 'But then we have a lot to put up with where men are concerned. I love Max very dearly, as indeed I should, but that doesn't prevent me from thinking of him on occasion as a royal pain in the ass, because that's sometimes what he *is*.'

'But you don't feel that way about him all the time.'

'Of course not. If I did I might get myself into trouble, as I suppose I have to say Mum did. Of course Alec wasn't married at that time but *she* was. And I expect you know Alec has glorious visions of his name in the New Year Honours List? . . . It wouldn't do his chances much good if his terrible guilty secret were to become common knowledge, especially with this other awful business and all that nonsense in the papers . . . I know these are enlightened times. But even so . . .'

'It *is* an awful business,' Dobie said. 'That's my only excuse.'

'For what?'

'For being so intrusive. Into private matters.'

'The worst of it is I can't feel I've been of any help at all.'

'I rather think you have. I'm sure that you have. Though just for the moment,' Dobie said, 'I can't see exactly how.'

Half an hour later, he still couldn't.

Something she'd said was important. That was all.

It would help, Dobie thought, if I knew *why* it was important. But all I really have is the sensation that there was something she'd said that *fits*. Or maybe doesn't fit. In either case, alters the pattern. Something that goes into place not like a piece in a jigsaw but like a keystone in an arch. Syllogism. A form of discourse in which, certain things being posited, something else follows from them by necessity. *If p then q. If q then r. Therefore, if p then r.* Elementary first-year Aristotelian logic. *No M is P. Some S is M. Therefore, some S is not P.* Categorical, my dear Watson. The only trouble with mathematical logic is that sooner or later it drives you round the bend. Unless of course you happen to be a computer. *O happy little IBM, he doesn't give a damn. I wish I were an IBM.* At least I've got the use of one. That's the next best thing.

In Sammy's room . . .

Preoccupied thus with his inner musings (thoughts you could scarcely call them), Dobie drove sedately back to 221B or rather to 12 Ludlow Road, where, as he made his way down the passage towards the staircase, various snuffling and sneezing sounds emanating from the inner sanctum on the right enabled him cogently to deduce that Watson's morning consultancy session wasn't yet concluded. Dobie entered his own sanctum – it was really *his* room now, not Sammy's – and seated himself at the computer with a certain air of confident deliberation, rather as a fighter jock might seat himself at the controls of a Tomcat; there were many things that Dobie wasn't very good at but the monitor screen was his element, just as the cirrus-streaked sky was the interceptor pilot's. The problem, of course, was to get himself safely up there. He carried out an unhurried instrument check and then began to prepare the machine for take-off.

He was still sitting at the end of the runway when Kate came in.

'What are you doing?'

'Just fooling around,' Dobie said.

'No, you're not. Should I leave you to it?'

'It's all right.' Dobie SAVE'd the set of equations he'd run up, though they differed in no important respect from Sammy Cantwell's, and pushed his chair back. 'I'm just programming information, that's all.'

'Good,' Kate said, yawning prodigiously and stretching herself out in the nearer armchair. 'Or it is if it helps to take your mind off things. You went out, didn't you? . . . Lucky sod. I hate having to run the clinic these summer mornings. I keep looking out the window and wishing I were somewhere outside.'

'Yes,' Dobie said. 'I was just thinking about that.'

'About me? Highly gratifying, I'm sure.'

'About your looking out the window. And about something else that chap told me.'

'Oh.' Kate rubbed her face gently, as though her cheek muscles had suddenly tired. '. . . No. My telepathic receiver's out of action. *What* chap?'

'The security bloke,' Dobie said. 'He was on about a funny thing that happened the day before Sammy got the sack. Apparently Jane Corder spoke to Sammy and afterwards he denied it. Well, and then *you* said you'd once seen Jane standing outside this place. Waiting.'

'*I*'ll tell you about a funny thing, Dobie. When I saw you poking away at that machine, I thought you were giving all that side of things a rest. Because Jacko's right, you know. You really ought to.'

'Supposing,' Dobie said, 'Jane knew that Sammy was lending someone his room . . . and what for . . . I'm thinking that *she* might have told him to stop doing it. She was the boss's wife, after all. He'd probably have reckoned he'd better do what he was told, and by the same token he could have been embarrassed enough about it not to want to admit to the conversation afterwards. And then remember the message he left for you. *I won't be able to help any more because of something else that happened at Corders* – wasn't that what he said? . . . It all fits . . .'

'But why should Jane care a damn *what* he did with his room? It wasn't any of her—'

'She might have cared if she'd known that Jenny

was one of the people using the room. Jane was quite possessive about her friends. And don't forget she wanted to see me about something, about something she said was private. You see what I'm getting at?'

'You think she meant to tell you what Jenny was getting up to.'

'It seems fairly likely.'

'But then she'd have known who she was meeting here.'

'You're catching on.'

'And . . . that's why she's dead?'

'You're catching on *fast*. She couldn't be allowed to tell me. Or anyone else.'

'But it still doesn't make sense. If people started killing people for knowing about things like that, nobody'd be safe. I mean, supposing *I*'d seen them going in or coming out . . . I didn't, of course, but I might have . . .'

'Exactly,' Dobie said. 'So there has to be more to it than that. And so there is. Because *if* you'd seen them, you wouldn't just be tying them to each other. You'd be tying them to Sammy as well.'

'And so to . . . ?'

'Exactly,' Dobie said again. 'Adultery's not such a very serious matter, except to the people concerned. But, as Inspector Jackson says, murder is.'

Kate got up and went for a little walk, to the far end of the room and back again.

'. . . Well, the one thing you *haven't* been doing is giving it a rest. That's obvious.'

'I've been programming information. Like I said.'

'You don't mean . . . ?'

'Here.' Dobie flicked at the keyboard and the monitor screen came to life, flashing blurred symbols at him with an eye-baffling velocity before settling down to show a bewildering jumble of intersecting triangles. Kate stared at it, waiting for the pattern to change. But it didn't.

'That's information?'

'That's a syllogistic series,' Dobie said, 'expressed in terms of Lorenzian equations. Of course I haven't taken it very far as yet.'

'And that's how you scrape a modest living? Setting up that kind of thing?'

'I and a few other like-minded citizens. Mostly in the States. Of course a computer is only as good as its programs and that's where I've got a bit lucky, because I received some of the most advanced programming that's ever been developed only last week. Would you like to see one?' Dobie took a mini-disc from the brown paper envelope on the desk and slid it into the machine. '. . . What we're hoping eventually to get is a mathematical representation of the whole of physical reality. A set that includes all conceivable sets. In fact that's theoretically unachievable because of the Lorenz effect, but by seeing where and why we fail we can maybe track down all those strange attractors a little more closely. So we start off *here* . . .'

Kate's mouth came a little open as she stared at the screen. On the right-hand side, a jet-black ball bisected by the edge of the monitor extended a long curved jet-black tentacle rimmed with golden fire. The fire grew in intensity, reaching back to touch the dark sphere itself which also began to glow; it might have been a planet eclipsing a brilliant sun that now stood on the point of emergence. The arm of darkness began to curve back, starting to form a circle as the monitor tracked towards it.

'. . . Looks a bit like a Star Wars scenario, doesn't it?' Dobie's voice said comfortably. 'That's in fact what the Americans are using it for. Among other things.'

The dark ball was disappearing from view as the monitor rushed on towards the centre of that huge dark loop which had begun to glitter now with points and whorls of colour, red and blue and green and yellow; within the loop another loop was forming, and then another, the colours growing always brighter, clearer.

'. . . I suppose you could say we're making a map of the furthest reaches of the human mind, though I don't think George Campbell would put it quite that way. He'd say we were expressing a finite set series in terms of a unified field theory . . . but that's only saying the same thing in a different way . . .'

His voice seemed to murmur into Kate's ears from a great distance away as the circle of blazing light into which she was rushing exploded suddenly outwards in a shower of symmetrical particles and another long arm of light came round to envelop her, thrusting out other curving arms like the whorled shells of DNA spirals, failing to clutch her and detain her as she sped onwards towards the centre of another spinning spiral like that of a bursting nebula; she heard her own voice murmur in reply, 'But it's so *beautiful* . . .'

Still the hallucination held as the nebular pattern widened out into dense white clouds of primal matter through which strange never-before-seen shapes and colours danced like jewels, like snowflakes, forming millions of widening circles like those made by raindrops on water.

'I *told* you it was,' Dobie said. 'But you didn't believe me. Not that I blame you. People usually don't.' He touched the keyboard and the screen went blank, went dead, and Kate went on staring at it, feeling a sadness, the sadness of a deprivation.

'You know, for the first time I feel a bit sorry for Jenny.'

'Why?'

'I don't see how any woman could compete with *that*.'

'Oh well,' Dobie said. 'I always thought that Jenny was beautiful, too.'

'But you didn't *make* her. Like you made that, that . . . *that.*'

'I didn't exactly *make* it, you know. It's more like translating a language. And the computer does most of it, anyway, because once you've fed it the basic sets it'll generate all the others that follow from the same premises and it'll fit them all in the places where they should go. Of course, even so . . . it takes time.'

'How much time?'

'We've been working for about twelve years on that one.'

It takes a lot of time and a lot of patience. But by six o'clock that evening Dobie felt ready to engage the dialogue mode.

ACCEPT CONSTRUCTION
JOHN IS AN ORPHAN Q JOHNS PARENTS ARE DEAD
ACCEPT CONSTRUCTION
JOHNS PARENTS ARE DEAD BUT YOURS ARE ALIVE
NEGATE CONSTRUCTION
JOHN IS AN ORPHAN BUT YOURS ARE ALIVE
BY ESTABLISHING ANAPHORIC IRREGULARITY

The computer made a faint humming noise indicative of willing obedience and then answered:

OK

Dobie coded in and continued:

ACCEPT CONSTRUCTION
I AM A WIDOWER Q MY WIFE IS DEAD
ACCEPT CONSTRUCTION
MY WIFE IS DEAD BUT YOURS IS ALIVE
ANALYSE CONSTRUCTION
I AM A WIDOWER BUT YOURS IS ALIVE

The computer immediately decided

CONSTRUCTION UNACCEPTABLE BVO ANAPHORIC GAP

Dobie coded again and instructed it to

ELIMINATE GAP

The computer sighed audibly.

NO CAN DO

it said.

CONFIRM (Dobie politely suggested) ANAPHORIC GAP AS BVO PARADOX

This actually took the computer several seconds.

CONFIRMED GAP AS BVO OUX-EKON-EKON TYPE PARADOX OK OK OK

To be or not to be, Dobie thought. He sat back in his chair and took several deep breaths, this in order to oxygenate his brain. The computer's brain required no oxygen and the computer therefore did nothing. Nothing at all. Dobie stared at it in silence for a few minutes before attacking the keyboard again.

YOURE PISSING ME OFF

he typed. To this the computer wittily replied

FUCK YOU TOO

and added several asterisks by way of emphasis. The programme was one that allowed Dobie to express his feelings on occasion and further permitted the computer, though it didn't have any feelings, a purely nominal right of reply. This emotional safety-valve was Dobie's own innovation; it was pleasant after six or eight hours of labour to be able to relieve in this wise his frustration and it made no difference to the computer either way.

Clearly it was back to the drawing-board. He didn't need the computer to tell him there was a paradox somewhere in the programming, an anaphoric gap; he needed it to tell him where it was, so that he could eliminate it. There had to be a way in somewhere but he couldn't see it and the computer couldn't see it either. Well, it was early days yet. Far too early, really, to be losing your temper. It wasn't the computer's fault. The computer wasn't losing its temper. Maybe that's the whole trouble. *That*'s why NO CAN DO.

Dobie got up from his chair and began to walk to and fro, to and fro, to and fro. The key to the whole thing, he thought, is what somebody *feels*. That's why I can't solve the conundrum. I haven't felt anything very much since Jenny got dead and I probably didn't feel enough before. Not enough to understand anything. Not the computer's fault and not Jenny's; no, mostly mine. Now all that rather frightening yet welcome numbness is wearing off, I'm starting to hurt. I'm starting to get angry. Maybe I *need* to lose my temper if I'm ever to find the answer to this one. Because the answer has to have a human form and because that's how that certain human form is always managing to stay ahead of me. Pushed ahead by anger. Or hatred. Or something like that. But anger at what? Hatred of whom? If I don't feel those things, how can I tell?

He sat down again at the computer, went back to the graphic mode and started out again. Building on the screen a circle of fact, an ellipse of theory, moving the two shapes this way and that, trying to get them to coincide. Once he had found a point of coincidence, he'd move them round their common epicentre at an increasing speed until they began to fluctuate, to spin off course. Then he'd have pinned it down. The strange attractor. Or at least have established its location. But it would all take time. It would take a lot of time and a lot of patience.

At nine o'clock Kate brought him in his dinner on a tray and he left the computer in order to eat it. She sat down again in the armchair to watch him eat it; he seemed to be pretty hungry but there was that in his appearance which precluded the asking of silly questions, such as *How's it going?* She waited instead for him to speak first, which he didn't do until he'd finished eating. Then he went at once back to the computer, carrying his coffee-mug, and lit a cigarette. She'd already noticed the twelve or fifteen crumpled stubs in the ashtray and that had surprised her a little; Dobie wasn't usually a heavy smoker. He looked all right, though, on the whole. Not even particularly tired. Just a little crumpled up, like the cigarette stubs.

'I can't tell you,' he said. 'Not yet.'

'No progress to report?'

'It isn't like that. Either you're through or you're not through. You're inside or you're outside. It's like hacking, in a way.'

'Hacking?'

'Getting into someone else's computer. Only this is getting into someone else's brain. Seeing the patterns the way another person sees them. Tricky.'

It wasn't the kind of mental activity that Kate could even begin to imagine. She got up and looked over Dobie's shoulder at the monitor screen, to see if that helped. It didn't. The inside of your brain apparently looked like thousands and thousands of intersecting parallelograms, all shifting restlessly about. It wasn't, surely, a picture that any neuro-surgeon would recognise. 'It reminds me of a Chinese box,' she said. In so far as it reminded her of anything.

'We'd have a Chinese box turned inside out in a matter of milliseconds.' He didn't sound contemptuous. Just flatly dismissive. 'It's a lot more complex than that.'

'I suppose it would be.'

'Maybe you could say the symbols I'm using are something like characters in a drama. They don't stay put, you see. They move from place to place. Until,' Dobie said as flatly as before, 'they're terminated. And even then they go on affecting the pattern, although they're not there.'

'The butterfly effect?'

'On a magnified scale.'

'Extraordinary.' But Kate wasn't contemptuous, either. She was fascinated. 'Which one is *me*?'

'It doesn't work like that, either. The characters aren't *really* characters, they're only arrangements of syllogistic series, actual and potential. From one point of view, all right, that's what *we* are, or that's how we are as a computer sees us. But it's still only a metaphor. Even when you've picked out a significant pattern, it still has to be interpreted. That's normally a job for the physicists. I'm not a physicist.'

'No. In fact I can't quite make out *what* you are. There's one thing,' Kate said, 'you've never asked me. Perhaps you should.'

Dobie didn't raise his head. 'About you and Sammy?'

Kate sighed. 'The answer is no. We didn't.'

'We see that situation in terms of unrealised potential. So I'll check that out as confirmed.'

Kate didn't hit him. Instead, she sighed again. 'Unrealised potential. That's me, folks.'

'That's *everybody*,' Dobie said. 'The way a computer sees us. Computers can attain their potential. People can't. That's why I can't foretell the future with this thing. All I can do is analyse. I can't predict.'

'. . . What's *our* potential, Dobie?'

'I have a feeling,' Dobie said, 'that it might be quite considerable.'

'Uh-huh. But that's a feeling? Not a prediction?'

'It's an intuition.'

'Dobie, there's hope for you yet.'

'Yes, indeed,' Dobie said. 'For both of us.'

'Is there anything else I can get you?'

'Not right now,' Dobie said. His head was lowered over the keyboard again. He heard the door close behind her as she left the room. If it is possible for a door to close light-heartedly, that one did.

Of course light-heartedness is a part of it. Euphoria, even. There have to be moments when everything seems to be going good, the patterns falling into place, the fingers moving on the keyboard as though guided by predestiny. But euphoria won't sustain you for long. It comes and it goes. You need something else to push you through the long dark hours when the mind is numbed and the fingers move as though clogged in a morass of self-doubt; you need anger, you need hatred. Things like that. When his fingers came to a temporary halt Dobie got up from his chair and walked round the room, his hands behind his back, with the tape on the cassette-player once again turning and Oscar Petersen's turmoiled arpeggios once again accompanying the confusion of his thoughts, Oscar Petersen's agile fingers replacing his on that other keyboard, the walls of his brain echoing to those elaborately devised chord progressions. As he walked slowly up and down, letting his anger grow . . .

Because he knew this wasn't the usual enemy. This time he wasn't up against some elusive mathematical abstraction, some concept lurking behind a thicket of Dirac equations; much less up against George Campbell's battery of square-eyed whiz-kids in downtown Boston, all intent on flushing the bird from the thicket and shooting it dead before the goddam Limeys had loaded their shotguns. This was a bird of a different feather, another kind of enemy. This was N. An enemy who had stolen Dobie's wife and had later killed her and who was thus no longer an enemy but *the* enemy, Pluto to Dobie's ineffectual Orpheus. And this room, Sammy's room, was the dark-shaded Hades to which Jenny had been rapt; she too had lain on the bed with another head beside hers on the pillow, listening idly to this same cunning music, and through that recollected music had sent her husband some kind of a message, perhaps of joy, perhaps of despair, who could tell? Now here he was in the underworld, feeling oddly at home here as probably she had also, marching soundlessly up and down, letting his anger build and build before sitting at the computer desk to send out messages of his own, tapping out the codes and symbol strings, trying to shape the outline of a face, the face of the head on the pillow.

Oh yes, this bird had a face. N had a face. A face that Dobie hated, though he couldn't see it. He *had* to hate it in order to get to see it. He wanted to see it because he hated it. Not that seeing it would be enough. There was a key on the computer board that he hadn't yet used. A key marked CANCEL. That would do the trick . . .

But he wasn't just a transmitter of messages. Very far from it. He was a receiver as well. Behind the insistent interchange of the piano and the guitar he could hear no less insistent voices, other people's voices and sometimes his own, voices creating other random patterns in his mind as his feet moved back and forth across the carpet, the voices and the rhythmic tread of his feet combining at times with the insidious water-trickle of the music,

It was great fun
But it was just one of those things . . .

and at other times overcoming it, erasing it briefly from the tape until with the cessation of the voices it could return . . .

It's like going over the top of a hill. All of a sudden, there's nothing to stop you . . .

He kept the pistol in the chest of drawers, under his shirts . . .
He's hardly been to see me at all this past month . . .
When you're that age, it's quite easy to mistake the nature of a relationship. I suppose at any age, for that matter . . .
Now that I know him quite well, I'm sure he really was in love with her . . .
I always thought that Jenny was beautiful, too . . .

His own voice was one of the voices but sounding different, hollow, as though echoed from the dark water at the bottom of a deep, deep well, and other echoes seemed to be mingled with it, the distant murmur of a string quartet, the vibrating rumble of an approaching aircraft. While behind those background reverberations the voices kept on speaking.

She kept it hidden away . . .
But he lied about it, just the way he lied about everything else . . .
Something like characters in a drama. They don't stay put. They move from place to place . . .

One voice, though, that he couldn't hear clearly, couldn't recall distinctly enough. A very important voice. It was lucky that he'd run off a copy of the tape. He went to the cassette-player and exchanged Oscar Petersen for Sammy Cantwell, the slow dark piano chords for the stumbling monotonous voice, *there was an unpleasantness, y'know?* . . . playing and rewinding the tape five or six times until the memory of that voice was part of the other memories and the voice part of those other voices that spoke together, interrupting one another confusedly:

. . . Something else had happened at bloody Corders . . . .

. . . The clinic's been broken into on three separate occasions lately . . .

. . . keys . . . keys . . . I have to know about the keys . . .

. . . because the keys, he thought, are the key to the case. The key to this room and the key to my flat and the key to the tune of the Cole Porter lyric. The black and white keys of the piano and the keys of Jane's red-ribboned typewriter. And the flat blank door of the monitor screen, still waiting to be opened . . .

Four o'clock in the morning. Time to reopen the dialogue. Dobie flexed his fingers over the keyboard and tried again.

If at first you don't succeed . . .

ACCEPT AGENT N Q TERMINATING SERIES SEQUENCE F
CONFIRM AGENT N Q TERMINATING SERIES SEQUENCE G

Can do, the computer decided. It sent

CONFIRMED

Dobie sent

CONFIRM AGENT N Q TERMINATING SEQUENCE H

The computer gave the matter some serious thought and then decided,

CONFIRMED

Dobie was beginning to feel tired. He ran the routine check on the programme's logical structures and syntactical rôle and found both to be impeccably intact. So there it was. A three-way terminator took you way beyond the bounds of possible coincidence, though of course never quite. For anyone but a computer, though, you could call it a certainty. No longer an assumption. The same person each time. N had killed all three. Four o'clock in the morning, though, and the face was still hidden behind the thicket. It had moved no closer. Dobie moved the monitor arrow to the panel marked

KILL

and pressed the button. The letters flickered into nothingness and the graphic mode returned. The pattern of the Chinese box had shifted. It looked very like a fluctuation. Dobie stared at the screen, not liking what he saw.

Seven fifteen a.m.

Kate came in, wearing a bright red flannel dressing-gown and carrying a teapot on a tray. This she almost dropped when she saw Dobie hunched up in his chair, still navigating the computer. 'My God, Dobie, haven't you been to bed *at all*?'

'Bed at all?' Dobie said dozily. 'No, I haven't been to bed at all, I've been . . . Don't worry about it. I'm used to staying up all night.'

'You'd better tickle your tastebuds with this lot,' Kate said crossly, plonking the tray down beside him on the work-table. 'And then come and have some breakfast. And then get some sleep. This is bloody ridiculous.'

'Don't want breakfast.' Dobie levered his eyes away from the monitor screen and peered vaguely round about him. 'Can't stop now we're on a roll.'

'On a *roll*? That thing's going to curl up and die on you if you work it like that. I'll report you to the Society for Prevention of Cruelty to Computers.'

'There isn't one.'

'There ought to be.' In fact he looked pretty much the same as when she'd left him last night. Somewhat distrait, but not noticeably the worse for wear. The room was full of tobacco smoke, though; he had to have got through a whole packet. She went to draw the curtains and open the window; another clear bright morning, with a few early starters scurrying earnestly along the pavements. 'Don't you ever get tired?'

'You get tired around the twelve-to-fourteen hour mark.' Dobie was prepared to be factual about this. 'You keep on working and then it's all right. It's a bit like the pain barrier for a distance runner. But I'm going to run into another one about two hours from now. Do you have anything that'd help to get me through it?'

'Breakfast would help,' Kate said firmly.

'I'll need something with a bit more kick to it than eggs and bacon.'

'I suppose you could shoot some Bennies if you wanted to. But *why* do you want to? What's the *hurry*?'

'I don't want to,' Dobie said. 'I *have* to.'

There are some patients it's no good arguing with. It does more harm than good. Kate went to fetch the Benzedrine tablets from the refrigerated medicine cabinet at the back of her pantry and on her way through the kitchen clicked the switch to boil up another kettleful of water. When she got back Dobie was talking to the computer again, his lips moving as he fed it more mouthfuls of delicious information. The computer was getting breakfast all right. 'You'd better take them now if you're going to take them at all. Let me feel your pulse first.'

Nothing wrong there. Slow and steady.

Dobie said, 'What would have the opposite effect to these?'

'Depressant, you mean?'

'Narcotic. Something that'd send me off to sleep.'

'Valium. Or one of the derivatives. But I'm not giving you anything like that on top of the other. Let me know when you're on a down and I'll come and hit you on the head with a hammer.' No. Not funny. '. . . What *is* it, Dobie?'

'I don't like some of the results that I've been getting,' Dobie said, popping a couple of the little blue pills with effortless ease. 'One of the sequences I've been running . . . I don't like it at all.'

'What do you mean, you don't *like* it?'

'It looks as though another termination situation is going to arise. It looks as though that situation is imminent.'

'If you mean what I *think* you mean—'

'Then somebody's in danger,' Dobie said. 'Somebody else is due to go and there's not an awful lot I can do about it.'

'Because you don't know who it is?'

'Exactly. I can't tell who it is.'

'And when you say *go* . . . ?'

'Yes,' Dobie said.

Kate turned her attention towards the screen, where a small green circle was spinning on its axis. Spinning very slowly. But spinning. 'Bloody hell,' Kate said. 'You can't *know* that. You said yourself it couldn't predict.'

'It's not a prediction. It's a probability estimate. But ranking very high on the scale.'

'*How* high?'

'Almost as high as it'll go. It's the time factor that's, well . . . crucial.'

'So what *can* you do?'

'Go on working,' Dobie said. 'Trying to clear up a little point here, a little point there. Like what happened to Jane Corder's clothes.'

'Jane Corder's *clothes*? She was wearing them.'

'Not when *I* saw her she wasn't.'

Kate gave it up. 'Is there anything I can do to help?'

'You can help the cause of suffering humanity down

there in the clinic. While I go on fighting this many-headed hydra here.'

'A man's gotta do what a man's gotta do.'

'Yup,' Dobie said.

Of course it wasn't really a fight. Or even a race, because once inside the computer time had no meaning. The computer didn't understand about death, the enemy with no face at all; it had no sense of urgency. But Dobie did, and when around half-past nine the fatigue hit him it was that alone which kept him going; the Benzedrine helped only a little and the taped music no longer helped him at all, was lost in the thrumming roar of the traffic going by outside which impacted upon Dobie's eardrums with the thundering force of Pacific breakers. When he got up to close the window he found himself barely able to stand upright; when he went back to his chair his hands were trembling so wildly he could no longer control the computer keys. Luckily he'd been through all this before and had the computer self-programmed against this eventuality; it went on working busily as he sat there in a semi-blinded haze, waiting for the cloudiness that affected his vision and the jerkiness that affected his movements to go away, to yield to the inexorable pressure of his will-power and once again recede. While in the computer's unbefuddled brain the patterns kept forming and re-forming.

Until in the end the noisy traffic's boom was quietened and the ache at the base of his skull was eased and Dobie's fingers moved to the keyboard again; day and night, night and day were all the same to him now. His mind was at last free of all thought, of all speculation, of hatred and of anger; he was back inside the computer again, part of its millionfold function, and there was no longer any hurry, and cause for alarm or need for regret . . .

He was through.

4

Pontin was engaged the while in one of his favourite pursuits. Reading the morning papers. As a concession to the varied pressures exerted upon him in consequence of the recent stirring events in his manor he had spent little more than five minutes on the sports pages and various other third-page allurements before turning briskly to what quite a number of the tabloid editors clearly considered to be the meat of the day's matter. Headlines that seemed, however vaguely, to relate to the affair of the Cardiff Multiple Murderer were at any rate prominent; their tone varied from the mildly speculative (as with the *Spook*'s wistful inquiry, IS JACK BACK?) to the altogether more boisterous (MANIAC SEX KILLER STILL ON THE PROWL, according to the *Daily Strip*). Pontin was most displeased to observe that despite the lengthy interview he had afforded yesterday to the gentlemen of the press his photograph did not appear in any of these influential organs of opinion; an unflattering likeness, however, of That Man Dobie (as Pontin thought of him) had been reproduced in several (COLLEGE PUNDIT MYSTERY WITNESS TO BRUTAL SLAYINGS). Well, Pontin was well accustomed to this sort of thing. He was after all the Strategist, the Seasoned Hand, the Man behind the Scenes. Not for him the nerve-tautening tension of the scraped matchflame illuminating the face of the pockmarked gentleman in the slouch hat, the shots ringing out in the night as the Bugatti spins out of control, whizzing off the topmost bend of the Grande Corniche. No. For him, the telephone buzzer, the piled folders of the office desk. And, of course, page three of the *Daily Strip*. Immersed in awestruck contemplation, he came to himself abruptly as someone rapped sharply on the office door. 'Come in,' he said. 'Oh, it's you, Jackson.'

Jackson advanced. 'I believe you sent for me, sir.'

'Take a seat. Take a seat. Jackson?'

'Sir?'

'What's a pundit?'

'I think it's one of them Indian geezers, sir, as comes up and strangles you from behind.'

'Ah. Yes, that sounds very likely. Well now, what can I do for you, Jackson?'

'You sent for me, sir.'

'I did? . . . Oh yes. Yes. Right. We got to get things *moving*, Jackson. Time we fingered someone on this Dobie business.'

'Yessir. In fact I just had a call from Mr Dobie. I've arranged to meet him—'

'I'm not interested in *arrangements*, Jackson. I'm interested in *arrests*. I've been reading these autopsy reports very carefully, very carefully indeed, and I'm not satisfied, I'm not satisfied at all. I don't believe this Dr Coyle knows her butt end from her knucklebone.'

'Yes,' Jackson said. 'It's the time factor that's, well . . . crucial.'

'Quite so. It's her estimate of the time of death of that Dobie woman that's been holding us up, right? And from what you tell me, Dobie's shacking up with her right now. It's a case of barefaced collusion if I ever came across one. We've got to break this so-called medical evidence, Jackson, if we want to get anywhere. I wouldn't set much store by it at the best of times.'

'And how are we going to set about doing that, sir?'

'Bring her in for questioning, of course. I'll soon put her through the hoops. Find out just what it is she's been up to with that . . . that . . . *pundit*.'

'If you say so, sir.'

'I do so say so, Jackson.'

'I'll send someone round right away.'

It wasn't a job that Jackson fancied himself; Kate Coyle, as he knew from past experience, could be quite a formidable bit of crumpet when she got her Irish up. Besides, he had an appointment and was now in some danger of arriving late. Foxy Boxy was nowhere in sight that morning so he deputed Detective-Constable Grimwade to execute this tricky mission. 'Just ask her if she'd be good enough to accompany you to the station – you know – be *tactful* about it. And you needn't be in too much of a rush to get there. She won't be through with her patients till half-past twelve at the earliest.'

'Rely on me, sir,' Grimwade said.

Jackson got into his car and scooted off.

The colourful columns of that morning's daily press had stimulated other imaginations beside Pontin's and there was still a fair-sized crowd surrounding the Corders' house when he arrived. The front door was opened to him by a dark-haired girl who frowned down at him mistrustfully. 'Miss Corder? . . . Detective-Inspector Jackson. I spoke to you on the phone.'

'You're late,' Wendy said. 'Mr Dobie's been here these past ten minutes. He's in the sitting-room if you'd like to join him.'

'Yes, I'm sorry. I was unavoidably—'

'And now *I'm* late. I have to get to work. Make sure the door's locked behind you when you leave, if you don't mind?'

More than a touch, Jackson thought, of her father's well-known energetic irascibility. He watched her head towards the garage with long athletic strides, then turned and went through the hallway into the sitting-room, having taken due care to close the front door behind him. Dobie, he saw, had ensconced himself in the alcove at the far end of the room beside the cocktail bar; in his rôle of mystery witness he had seemingly adopted an interesting windblown appearance, as though someone had just pulled him backwards through a giant hair-dryer. His ears that morning didn't seem quite to fit. As a result, his glasses were poised on his nose at a lopsided angle. Leaning forwards as into the teeth of a hurricane, he saluted Jackson with a cordial handshake before falling back into the sofa cushions with a curious rolling motion, like that of a dying duck in a thunderstorm. 'Are you feeling all right, Mr Dobie?' Jackson inquired.

'I'm fine. Just didn't get too much sleep last night.'

'Ah.' Jackson sat down cumbrously. 'You're letting these things prey on your mind, perhaps. You don't want to do that if you can help it.' The sofa was certainly a good deal more comfortable than it appeared to be. Lapped in upholstered luxury he surveyed the sitting-room, which looked very much as it had looked before. 'Now may I ask why you've brought me here, sir? Some other aspect of the matter, maybe, as you feel you'd like to talk to me about?'

'I thought we should take another look at the scene of the crime,' Dobie said. 'Rather an apt phrase, that. I mean that's so exactly what it *was*.'

The mystery witness was clearly prepared to be as much of a mystery as usual. Jackson took out his handkerchief and blew his nose. 'I promise you, sir, we've been over this place very carefully. We may have been a mite remiss in the case of that Mr Cantwell but I don't think you'll find that there's much we've missed out on *here*.'

'Not you,' Dobie said. 'Me. It's almost the first thing I noticed when I sat down here that night and because it was so obvious I went and forgot about it. Don't *you* notice anything about this room?'

Jackson, at something of a loss, blinked about him. 'I can't say I do. It's all very nice and clean and tidy. Some expensive stuff, of course, in the way of furniture. But I don't see the point you're trying to make.'

'When I came into the room,' Dobie said, '*I* thought it looked rather like a stage set. You know, in a theatre. I only remembered that last night when I was trying to explain how a symbolic series works in a computer sequence. I said they were like characters in a drama. Which they're not, really, but I didn't see how else I could explain it.'

'You're not very *good* at explaining things, sir, if I may say so. I still haven't got the foggiest—'

'But it's *obvious*. What's the good of a drama without an audience?'

Jackson pondered on the matter. Enlightenment still refused to dawn. 'What sort of audience had you got in mind?'

'It's more what someone else had in mind. Someone thought that *I*'d make a pretty good audience. Someone made bloody sure that I *would* be. Set me down right here on this sofa, in the front row of the stalls so to speak, and then tied me hand and foot so that I'd have no choice but to stay there. Not a bad idea at that, but I don't think many contemporary managements would go to *that* extreme. The Theatre of Bondage, you might call it. It'll come, it'll come.'

'But what would be the *point* of this exercise?'

'I'm telling you,' Dobie said patiently. 'Someone wanted me to see the play.'

'Ah yes. Of course. The play.' Jackson looked once more around the room, wondering if he could subdue this pundit himself or if he wouldn't be better advised to summon assistance. 'Well, the missus quite enjoys a good

Agatha Christie now and again, a rat-trap or whatever it's called, but I myself—'

'I'd have to be drugged, though,' Dobie said, 'before I could be tied up. Otherwise I might have objected to such a procedure. But a *sleeping* audience is no good to anyone – least of all Agatha Christie. So I'd need to be woken up, you see, before the play could begin. Luckily Agatha happened to know that a convenient curtain-raiser would be coming over from Paris at eight forty-five and that no one could go on sleeping through that racket. The time factor, you see, was crucial. And luck didn't really come into it. No. It was all planned.'

'Yes. So you say. But planned to what *purpose*?'

'Ah. I thought you'd never ask. Agatha wanted a *witness*, don't you see? – someone who'd tell *you* that Jane had been killed here, in her own home, by some unknown intruder. In fact, of course, she wasn't.'

'She wasn't?'

'No. She'd been killed all of forty-five minutes earlier, when she got to my flat. She didn't know that our arrangement had been changed, because she didn't change it. Agatha did. Just left a message for me with the college secretary. Nothing easier.'

'But look *here*,' Jackson said, gobsmacked. 'You yourself said—'

'I was deceived.'

'Oh.'

'I didn't suspect anything. Why should I have? I showed up here, read the little note Agatha had prepared for me, had a little drink and passed out. I don't know exactly what was in the whisky, Kate says it may have been some kind of valium derivative but it was pretty strong . . .'

'Lab says there was nothing wrong with the whisky.'

'Well, that was never a serious problem. I mean, I was out cold. Agatha would have got back from my place by half-past eight at the very latest and have had plenty of time to truss me up and replace the whisky in the decanter. And when I came to . . . Well, there of course was Agatha, sitting over there in that armchair and wearing a borrowed raincoat and hat. Act One Scene One. The curtain goes up. Very dramatic.'

Jackson stared at the back of the armchair. Then made a floundering gesture with his right hand. 'Yes, but—'

'There's Agatha. And there's me. A captive audience in every sense of the word. But of course I can't *see* Agatha. Not properly. Not until Agatha gets up and exits stage right, and even then I can't register much more than the hat and the raincoat and dark trouser-legs. All I really have is a general impression of a male figure moving quickly out of sight and into the dressing-room.'

'The dressing-room?'

'The kitchen. It's more of an *un*-dressing-room, really. Because that's where the hat and coat come off and underneath them Agatha's wearing Jane Corder's clothes. Red blouse and dark trousers. It's all a bit like a Feydeau farce, one of those things where people are always whizzing in and out of each other's bedrooms disguised as Charley's Aunt. That's what Agatha does. Pops on Jane's raincoat instead of the other, puts on a blonde wig instead of the hat, goes out by the back door and comes in by the front, so that I think it's Jane just arriving. In the ordinary way I might have expected to have heard her car arriving, but what with the noise of that damned aeroplane . . . Oh, Jane's car was *there* all right, Agatha had driven it over from my place but of course she'd arrived much earlier, just left it in the garage. Anyway, like I said . . . I was deceived.'

'But how could you have been? You saw *her* all right.'

'Yes, I did. *And* heard her. She was calling my name. Of course I only saw her for a few seconds and I didn't have my glasses on . . . and because I was *expecting* to see Jane it never even occurred to me that it might be someone else. Even so, yes, it was a very good impersonation. Very good indeed. It *must* have been. After all, Agatha must have felt pretty confident about it. But the audience was a convenient distance away and it only had to be for a very short space of time. Just long enough for Agatha to move stage right again, out of sight of the audience, hit the door a bonk with her hand and make a gasping noise, grab the original hat and raincoat and skedaddle. All pretty simple, if you've got the nerve. Agatha has. And to spare.'

Jackson shook his head, like a horse ridding himself of a troublesome fly, and got up from the sofa. Moving with slow and measured paces he walked over to the hallway entrance, turned and walked to the kitchen door, opened it, closed it, came back and sat down once more on the sofa. 'For the life of me I still don't see—'

'Agatha likes playing games. Agatha's good at them. But this one isn't over yet, not by a long way. Because Jane's still on the bed in my flat. She has to be picked up and put in the sea if the whole charade's going to be convincing. So Agatha has to drive back there in her own car, return my wife's wig, put Jane's clothes back on her again, take her out to some lonely beach and dump her. And also take the raincoat and hat back to where they came from, because there's just the remotest chance they might be missed and Agatha doesn't leave *anything* to chance. The only trouble is, life isn't like that. Things *do* happen by chance. Like my wife getting back from Paris a day before she was expected. Agatha hadn't planned on killing Jenny. It was just a disagreeable necessity, when Jenny walked into the bedroom and found Jane's body there. Luckily Agatha had got back by then and was able to do something about it with the nearest thing to come to hand, which happened to be Jenny's typewriter. A case of panic stations, I rather fancy. And it put the timing all wrong. Agatha had counted on getting Jane away from my place long before I got back but it didn't work out that way. There was I, parking my car outside, and there was Agatha with *two* bodies in the bedroom. Logical thing to do would have been to set *me* out in the chorus line as soon as I came in through the door but Agatha didn't want to do that after setting me up as the witness to the other thing. No, I was just plain lucky there.'

'Be going a bit over the top, wouldn't it? With two corpses there already . . .'

'Oh well.' Dobie took off his glasses and wiped the lenses with the end of his tie. Devoid of their protection, his eyes looked tired and faded. 'You've got to understand we're dealing with someone who kills people without any compunction whatsoever. A moral imbecile, if you like. *Over the top* was your own expression, wasn't it? You go over the crest of a hill and the slope runs downwards. So you were right . . . Sammy Cantwell was the hilltop and the others just part of a syllogistic series. You were right and I was lucky. Agatha's very dangerous indeed.'

'Ah.' Jackson was gifted with a sudden acumen. 'Is that why you're telling me all this?'

'Of course. Because I still don't really know who Agatha is. I only know what Agatha *does*. And it scares me.'

'As well it might.'

'As well it might. Because what in fact Agatha does when I arrive is hide Jenny's body under the bed and then just step outside into the bathroom. And wait. So that when I walk into the bedroom, there's Jane stretched out on the bed, still without her blouse and slacks because Agatha's still wearing them, and what *I* do then, naturally, is rush off to the sitting-room to telephone the police. And while I'm doing that Agatha puts Jenny on the bed, carries Jane out through the French windows to her car and loads her into the boot, gets in and drives quietly off to that lonely beach I mentioned. Again, it was simple but it was *improvised*. That's the scarey part. Don't you think?'

'Yes. Well, I see what you mean. It's often hard to pin anything down on a criminal who keeps his head.'

Dobie put his glasses back on.

'That's right. There isn't very much in the way of proof. It happened like that because it couldn't have happened any other way. I've run every other conceivable sequence through the computer but it's no good. Nothing else works out.'

'There's one little detail that you haven't made quite clear.'

'Oh?'

'. . . Like what's *behind* all this shemozzle.'

'You mean the motive?'

'Yes.'

'For killing Jane?'

'Yes.'

'That's what *I*'d like to find out,' Dobie said. 'Because I have to go at this one back to front. I mean, if I can discover the *motive*, then I should be able to tell you who Agatha is. The trouble is I don't really know very much about homosexuality.'

'Homo—'

Jackson stopped with his mouth open, in the attitude of a soldier stricken with shell-shock. The telephone on the far side of the room had started to ring. Seeing that Jackson was making no move to answer it, Dobie got up and shambled wearily across. 'Hello . . . ? Dobie here.'

'Dobie? Oh.' The voice at the other end sounded familiar. 'Oh hello. Dickie Bird. Could I speak to Wendy?'

'She left about half an hour ago. She said she was going to work.'

'Oh, I see. Well, she hasn't got here yet. That's why I rang. To see if anything was wrong. I mean, there's a lot of work here and if she isn't coming in—'

Dobie put the phone down and turned towards Jackson. 'I think we'd better go,' he said.

'Go where?'

'In my car. I'll drive. Because we're going to break the speed limit. Better a civilian than a police inspector, wouldn't you say?'

'Break the . . . ? What for? Look, Mr Dobie—'

'Oh, come *on*,' Dobie said impatiently. 'It's that bloody time factor. It's gone crucial again.'

Twenty minutes to one.

He might have done better to have used the telephone. But he didn't know that and, in any case, there wouldn't have been anybody there to answer it.

Dr Coyle's clinic was now closed.

Grimwade climbed stolidly up the staircase.

He could hear no sound from the upstairs flat. Only the creak of the stair treads under his booted feet. It was quite dark in the old house and his eyes, accustomed to the sharpness of the sunlight outside, weren't yet adjusted to the pervading dimness. They didn't detect the slim and shadowy figure waiting for him at the head of the stairs. When they did, he had time only to open his mouth in mild surprise.

'Doctor—'

The long knife blade came at him out of the darkness, striking with a terrifying speed at the base of his throat. But he didn't see that, either. He stood quite still, making a peculiar gargling sound, not very loud. That was all.

'Agatha,' Jackson said.

'Yes?' Dobie slammed the car door shut.

'He's the one who used Cantwell's room? Who used to meet your wife there, the way you said?'

Dobie had started the engine almost with the same

movement. Already the car was rolling forwards. 'Yes,' he said. 'That's Agatha.'

'But he can't be a *he*. Surely you couldn't have taken a *man* for Jane Corder.'

Past the police guard and the gawping knot of spectators. Dobie shifting gear on the open road, pressing down on the pedal. 'Of course not. I never said it was a man.'

'But then how—'

'I realise now,' Dobie said, 'that Jenny probably wouldn't have been very interested in a *man*.' The speedometer needle already on sixty. And rising. 'And anyway, computers can't tell the difference between a man and a woman. It's one of their little failings.'

'Is *that* what you meant by . . . ?' Jackson checked himself again. 'You're not going on to tell me that you know now who Agatha *is*?'

'Yes,' Dobie said. 'Of course I do.' Eighty now. And *still* rising. 'That's why we're in a bit of a hurry.'

That was one way of putting it. Jackson glanced hurriedly towards the solid trunks of the trees that were hurling themselves at the fly-speckled windscreen and closed his eyes.

Dr Coyle sat at the work-table in Sammy's room. Very still, trying to keep control. To hold command over the thoughts, the series sequences that were whirling through her brain. Because that was important. It's important in these situations to keep your head. She told herself that, firmly. Then opened her eyes.

The letter was still on the table. Her hand was still on top of it. It wasn't a letter, really. More of a manic outpouring. Very hurriedly and badly typed, barely coherent in fact, and with a minuscule but nasty smear of blood, as she now saw, marking the edge of the sheet. That policeman's blood. In no way a distinguished piece of writing;

Agatha wouldn't have been proud of it. But then Agatha was up against it this time. Out-computed. Damn you, Dobie. I don't even know how you did it. Was that how it went? . . .

> Well damn you Dobie, the police have come so you know how I did it and why and even though I fixed it for the cop it has to be all over, I realise that. Yes, I thought Jenny was beautiful too and I loved her very much in a way that you cant understand and that bloody cumputer cant either. I knew I might have to get rid of her in the end but I never wanted to. Of course it wasn't really for the money even though we were starting to rake it in, Sammy got the stuff for me and Jenny took it over to Paris where she knew the right people and it was going fine so I just don't know what got into Sammy, he just got cold feet and he was going to blow the whistle so he had to be stopped. That's where it started and this is where it ends. It's always easy for a doctor, I mean it won't even hurt. Jenny didn't feel a thing, either, it was all so quick but I had to do it, she'd never have gone along with my getting rid of Jane like that, even though Jane knew she was coming here, Jane would have told you and everyone else the bloody old cow. She spoiled everything getting back early everything.

. . . Not a long letter. But long enough. The syringe lay on the table beside it. Already loaded. It was true that it wouldn't hurt. Kate Coyle sat very still, looking at it.

The telephone rang on Corder's office desk. Or more exactly, hummed very discreetly, Corder's being *that* kind of an office. Alec reached across and switched on the microphone. 'Yes?'

'Bird here. I'm afraid there's still no sign.'

'She hasn't . . . come? Well, it's dashed odd.'

'They told me she left your house, oh . . . almost an hour ago. So I was wondering—'

'*Who* told you?'

'It was Mr Dobie, actually.'

'*Dobie?* What the hell was *he* doing there?'

'I don't know. I didn't ask. I assumed he—'

'It doesn't matter. Could be the damned girl's met with some kind of accident.'

'That's just what I was thinking. In fact I was wondering—'

'Give her another ten minutes. Then call the police.'

Corder switched off the mike. He felt concerned. But irrationally concerned, more concerned perhaps than he should be. He sat back in his chair and thought for a few seconds before leaning forward again to dial Susan Strange's number.

There was no reply.

'. . . If you think I'm going to sign *that*,' Kate said, 'you're crazy.'

It was quite dark in Sammy's room, too, because the curtains had been drawn across the windows. Unlike Grimwade, though, she could see quite clearly the blade of the long thin knife that was catching what little light there was, tilted unpleasantly across the lap of the shadowy figure seated on the other side of the table. Naturally Kate had thought of screaming, but she knew that wouldn't do any good. No one had heard the shot that had finished off Sammy; no one would hear a scream, either. Unless of course she could get a window open. But there was no chance of that, either.

'It's all the same to me,' Agatha said. Agatha had a pleasant voice, reasonable, gently persuasive. 'It's typed on your machine, you know. And it's got your prints on it now. It's just to make things a little bit easier for both of us.'

'Dobie won't believe it,' Kate said.

'He may do. Let's hope he does. Because then he won't have to go, too.'

The pen was on the table, beside the syringe. Kate looked at it, feeling the pressure of a strange will-power, a strange attractor, urging her to pick the damned thing up and get it over with. Go on. Pick it up. Sign it.

'. . . Sign it.'

'I won't.'

Kate pushed her chair back and stood up. The other's head turned to follow the movement but quite calmly, imperturbably, a loose curl of fine blonde hair falling away from the high smooth forehead. 'You're being very silly.'

'You're going to kill me anyway,' Kate said, backing away towards the far wall. The other rose then from the chair to follow her, the knife held now at waist level, the blade a long cold sliver of light pointing outwards, aimed at the undercurve of Kate's breasts. 'Yes, but don't you see that this way it's going to *hurt*? And the other way . . . that's so *simple*. A little jab and you'll drop off to sleep, just like Dobie.' A soft but still surprisingly pleasant giggle. 'I think you're quite fond of Dobie, aren't you? Why not? So was Jenny. He's an interesting man. And there's no real need for *him* to die. Not if you behave.'

Kate had reached the wall now and was backing along it past the shelves, her hands behind her. She wasn't acting terrified. She *was*. As anyone else would have been. But it's important in these situations to keep your head. She told herself that, firmly, as her fingers brushed the metallic surface of the cassette-player directly behind her and pressed the *Play* switch. She moved then a little more quickly to her right as the spools began to turn and Agatha followed her, a little more quickly but still quite calmly, unhurriedly. Agatha was even smiling. Agatha liked playing games. This was fun. '*Hey, Kate*,' Sammy said suddenly from just behind her. '*This is Sammy* . . .' Agatha stopped smiling and turned round and the blade of the knife turned with her and Kate threw herself and all her weight, which wasn't very much, against her and took her off balance and knocked her to the floor. Unfortunately she couldn't do this without losing her own balance and joining her there. For a second they stared at each other, as if in amazement, then Kate, spitting in a most unladylike way, grabbed Agatha by the throat and started to throttle her. She knew this was a mistake but she didn't care. As Jackson would have said, her Irish was up.

Jackson now had his eyes tightly closed all the time and with what seemed to him to be good reason. That way he didn't see Dobie crash two red lights in succession at sixty miles an hour in his lunatic progress up the City Road, though he was aware of a confused blare of startled hooters sounding from behind. Immediate resignation from the Force now seemed to him to be the only honourable course of action, provided that he could manage to live so long. He emitted a low moan of sheer terror as Dobie took the Ludlow Road corner with a bright yellow wail of protesting brakes like Batman in a strip cartoon, centrifugal force all but carrying his passenger out through the side door, and pulled up finally outside the clinic, leaving twenty yards of black scorched-tyre marks on the road in the process. Opening his eyes at last in infinite relief, Jackson saw that the driver, too, was white as a sheet.

'Go on. Get up there. Quick,' Dobie said. 'I'm *bushed*.'

'How the bloody hell d'you think *I* feel?'

But Jackson none the less jerked the car door open and ran for the clinic entrance, achieving in fact a pretty good turn of speed. The further away he could get from Dobie the better, in his opinion.

Grabbing Agatha by the throat had indeed been a mistake. Agatha was tall and lithe and amazingly strong and, despite Kate's show of dander, had her grip effectively broken in a matter of seconds. If she hadn't dropped the knife when she fell and lost it temporarily from view, such contest as there was would have ended then and there. As it was, Kate was able to pull herself back and get halfway to her feet before the other's hands clawed wildly at her legs, ripping her skirt and tugging her down to the floor again. Rolling over and over in a tangled confusion of kicking feet and furiously flailing arms, they cannoned together into the work-table with an impact that almost knocked it flying and left Kate badly winded. All she could do for a moment was gasp wheezily for breath, and that moment was sufficient for her opponent to ram a knee against her midriff and so secure convincingly the upper berth. Kate hadn't expected her enemy to be so damned strong. Strong enough not to need the knife. Strong enough to knock her out with a clenched fist, if given the opportunity . . .

Now she had an opportunity. And that was what she did.

She stared for no more than a moment at Kate's flushed and upturned face. Her own expression was still calm, even contemplative and she wasn't even breathing deeply. Rising easily to her feet, she reached out across the table for the syringe. But the syringe wasn't there. 'Ah *shit*,' said Agatha Christie.

And,

'Oh my *God*,' said Jackson.

Even in the semi-darkness he could see that there wasn't much he, or anyone else, could do for Grimwade. Who sat semi-slumped against the wall, one leg extended and the other drawn up, near enough to the head of the stairs for the blood to have soaked through the carpet on the topmost treads. Jackson didn't touch the body or look at it for very long; he let out a loud and furious bellow and rushed onwards. Agatha heard that bellow and the echo of tramping feet and said something else, this time inaudible.

The syringe had rolled off the table and on to the floor and she had found it almost at once. She had it in her hand now and Kate was lying on her back six feet away, one knee lifted, most of her thigh invitingly revealed by the long tear in her skirt, but Kate was moving now, coming to, one hand scrabbling at the nap of the carpet in sudden alarmed recollection, and the running footsteps were thumping nearer and there wasn't time. The knife lay where it had fallen, over by the bookshelves; Sammy's voice still droned away, '*. . . I'll be paying you the rest of my back rent soon as I get back from London . . .*' and Agatha moved, crouched like a wrestler and quietly as a cat, to retrieve it. Still crouching there, she waited as Sammy's message came to an end and the tape spools spun on silence and the door flew open with a sudden bang to the violent impact of Jackson's foot. Agatha waited then no longer but face contorted with effort was through the door and striking within the space of a heartbeat, catching Jackson off balance from the recoil of his kick and spinning him back and sideways. It was the sideways movement which partially saved him, causing the knife point to make its entrance not under his ribs but just above one stiffened elbow, a glancing, twisting blow tearing through cloth and skin and flesh and twisting him yet further sideways as the blade slid through and out. 'Ow,' Jackson said.

Agatha went on down the passageway, not clumping along as Jackson had done but running bouncily, flexibly, with long athletic distance-devouring strides. Dobie, plodding ploughman-like up the stairs with an aching weariness slowing his every step, reached the top just in time to see a tall shadowy figure armed with a fearsome carving-knife bearing down on him like the wrath of God. Giving himself about as much chance as the Three Blind Mice, he squeaked appropriately; it looked like no kind of a match and it wasn't. He saw, peering apprehensively downwards through the misted lenses of his glasses, the knife commence its long curving approach on a trajectory that would inevitably end in the pit of his stomach, whiplash towards him at a nigh-incredible velocity and then flash past his right hip as Agatha in mid-lunge caught her foot on Grimwade's outstretched leg and lost her balance again, this time to rather more spectacular effect. If you are going to trip over someone's leg, it's not a good idea to do so at the top of a long and narrow flight of stairs. Such had been the vehemence of Agatha's thrust that she went past the top twelve steps without even touching them; she contacted the thirteenth, however, with a hefty thump that was accompanied by a rather sick-making snapping sound, and made subsequent substantial contact with the sixteenth, twentieth and twenty-second before reaching the bottom. Dobie, whose eyes were now tightly closed, plotted her vertiginous progress by ear alone.

Thunk . . .

Thunk . . .

Thunk . . .

Thunk . . .

Wallop . . .

Even that way, it had sounded pretty ominous.

Dobie, after a moment's consideration, decided that he had better adopt a more conventional method of descending the stairs. He did so, slowly and painfully. Then sat down on the bottom tread, mournfully regarding the body which lay, one foot cocked up against the banisters, contortedly at his feet. Through now sightless baby-blue eyes, Jane Corder stared back at him. It was all very sad, Dobie thought. All very sad and unnecessary.

And hard cheese on Alec.

Heavy footsteps were coming down the stairs behind him. Jackson was clutching his right arm; blood had soaked his coat sleeve and dripped from his dangling hand down to the floor. He had left a trail of nasty wet splashes all the way down the staircase. 'You'd better get that seen to,' Dobie said.

'Wow, she was *fast*.' Jackson didn't say it altogether unadmiringly. Halted beside Dobie and leaking like a tap, he too was staring down at the silent upturned face. The over-heavy make-up on the lips and around the eyes had smeared rather badly and there was blood, too, trickling thickly through the dishevelled blonde hair. It wouldn't trickle for long, though. She was dead all right.

'Who the hell *is* she?'

'You don't know her?'

'Never seen her before,' Jackson said.

'Yes, you have. She just looks different. That's all.'

Dobie reached down and with some reluctance pushed his fingers into the tangled mass of blood-spattered hair. He lifted it away and the hair beneath was dark and short and sleek. 'Amazing what a difference a wig makes,' Dobie said, 'when the face and the figure are pretty much alike. You know, I saw a photograph of Wendy with a bathing-cap on and I thought it was a photograph of Jane. Wendy looked much younger, of course, but with a bit of heavy make-up like Jane used to wear . . .'

'Younger?' Jackson seemed still to be partly stupefied. 'Of course she would be. She's the daughter. Of course I know her.'

'Daughters often do look like their mothers. As Susan Strange reminded me. And when it comes to an impersonation . . . they *know* them so well. No wonder she was confident. And by the way, where's Kate?'

'Kate?'

Dobie and Jackson looked at each other. Then Dobie went up the stairs almost as fast as Wendy Corder had gone down them. He found Kate standing by the table in Sammy's room, holding a syringe in her hand and looking at it in a bemused sort of way.

'Kate, are you all right?'

'Of course I'm all right. Let *go* of me, you idiot.'

About a minute later Dobie said, 'Oh, I forgot.'

'What?'

'Inspector Jackson. He needs some medical attention.'

'Okay,' Kate said. 'That's what we're here for.'

'All the same,' Jackson said severely, 'you didn't ought to have done it, Mr Dobie. We'd've *caught* her all right. That's what the police are here for, the appreciation of criminals.'

'Apprehension.'

'We nab the buggers anyway.'

'*I* didn't do it,' Dobie said. 'If anyone did, it was Grimwade. He tripped her up.'

'There you are, then,' Jackson said contentedly. 'Once a copper, always a copper. I only hope—'

'Keep *still*, then,' Kate said, making with the bandages.

Policemen, whatever they are here for, aren't nearly so impressive when stripped down to their undervests. But then college pundits, Dobie thought, probably aren't either. Wendy had been more than a match for him in every sense. With that lean pliant body and all that dynamic . . . well . . . *virility*. He hadn't known much about strange attractors and he still didn't but he thought he could now understand Jenny a little better and that, as he now knew, had been the whole object of the exercise. Once you've understood a theorem you can wipe the blackboard clean. But not before.

Jenny, he thought, had probably wanted some excitement. Chiefly that. And so, in a different way, had he.

Twenty years of college punditry is enough for anyone. He'd wanted some excitement but he hadn't known it. Well, he'd got it. Thanks to her.

'What I want to know,' Jackson said, disturbing him when on the point of merging his musings with the comfortable inchoateness of sleep, 'is what I'm going to tell the Superintendent. Just because she can't very well be taken to court don't mean I won't have reports to write and I've got to have some idea of what it was she was up to. Right now I haven't. Not *exact*, like.'

'She was a bloody terrifying woman,' Kate said, stabbing viciously at the roll of bandage with a safety-pin. 'And I'm *glad* she's dead. That beastly knife . . . Out of my own kitchen was where she got it from. The *bitch*.'

'That's as may be and I can understand your strength of feeling. But,' Jackson said, 'that doesn't tell me quite what I—'

'You've got that letter, haven't you?' Dobie said. 'You've read it?'

'Yes, but that's not . . . I mean it's a fake. Not a real confession.'

'She had to tell a lot of the truth, though, in order to make it convincing. They were stealing the stuff from Corder all right, she and Sammy between them. And Jenny was running it out to France and selling it there. Sammy *did* get cold feet when he got caught and so Wendy killed him. Jenny didn't know about that, in fact I doubt if she knew that Sammy was involved at all. She thought Wendy was getting all this material off her own bat. Wendy was working there, after all, and what's more was the boss's daughter. Jane's daughter as well, of course. As we've noticed.'

'Yes,' Jackson said, surveying Kate's handiwork and moving his arm experimentally up and down. 'Nice job, doctor. Thanks very much. But killing your own mother, now, that's a real nasty thing to do. *That*'s the part as I don't seem to be quite able to grasp.'

'Oh well, she *hated* her mother. And as far as I can see the feeling was just about mutual.' Discreet bumping noises could be heard from the passageway outside, where other of the boys in blue were supervising the carting away of Agatha's mortal body. Dobie listened drowsily to the oddly comforting sound of receding footsteps . . . Bump. Bump. Bump. Bump. Bump . . . and woke to find Inspector Jackson's better hand on his shoulder, shaking him quite roughly. 'Don't go to sleep *now*, Mr Dobie.'

'Oh yes. Sorry. Take the point.' Heavy weights now seemed to be glued to Dobie's eyelids but he struggled gamely to continue. He took the point. What was it? . . . Ah yes. 'The point is that Jane didn't know a thing about the industrial espionage business but she *did* find out that Sammy was lending his room to Jenny and Wendy two or three evenings a week, for purposes she could guess at all too easily, and she was pretty furious. Jane was rather a jealous sort of person, after all. Jealous of her friends. She must have suspected that Jenny had made friends with her in the first place just to have a chance of speaking to Wendy and *I* suspect that was probably quite true. So she thought of it as some kind of a betrayal, I suppose. She was going to let me know all about it and she spoke to Sammy about it, too. She told him to stop lending Wendy the room and that was a mistake because Sammy of course told Wendy so Wendy knew that Jane knew . . .'

Oh God, Dobie thought, I feel so *tired* . . .

'And so of course Jane had to be stopped from talking in the same way as Sammy. Wendy wouldn't have been worried about the lesbianism thing because in this day and age who cares a damn? – but if the security people at Corders ever got to make a connection between her and Jenny and Sammy, then the whole thing would be finished and that's why they were so concerned to keep their meetings here a secret, Jenny even wearing that blonde wig and all. I don't know if you follow what I'm saying?' His voice seemed to be wandering all over the place, going up and down and sideways in a most disconcerting way. He was on the down phase now from the Benzedrine, as was obvious. '. . . Because the crazy thing is that Wendy wasn't really in it for the money. Those trips to Paris were just to keep Jenny excited and interested and feeling she was in on something naughty. Sammy was the only one who wanted money. Wendy didn't. All she wanted, at any rate to start with, was her own back.'

Jackson's voice came to him from a long long way away. 'Who on?'

On whom, a small answering voice said from the back of Dobie's brain. The voice, which was that of a former college pundit, had also gone a long long way away and could now be ignored. 'On Alec. I can't help feeling that if you give that letter to one of your police psychoanalyst blokes he'll be a whole lot more than mildly interested. She hated her mother and conversely, she felt herself drawn towards her father but she knew that what he'd really wanted was a son and though she tried her very hardest she knew she'd never be able to live up to his expectations in that respect. I wouldn't be surprised if that isn't what got her into that lesbian kick, sex rôle confusion or something like that. But Wendy was a very jealous person, too. Just like Jane, in fact. Daughters are often like their mothers mentally as well as physically . . . which is something else that Susan Strange told me.'

'Who *is* Susan Strange? You mentioned her before.'

'Oh, she's Alec's *other* daughter. Illegitimate, apparently. You could say that Susan started the whole affair when she came to live in Cardiff . . . in the same way you could say that Grimwade finished it. Without knowing anything at all about it. Because Alec started visiting her often and spending his free time in her house, I think he enjoyed her company and that isn't hard to understand because she seems to be a very nice person. Uncomplicated. Straightforward. Which, whatever else you can say of her, Wendy isn't. Or wasn't. She was like I said – jealous. Really badly miffed about it all. She knew Alec was in line for a peerage if his new hearing-aid devices got off the ground and she reckoned that if she could put a spoke in *that* little wheel it'd just about serve him right. So she set about doing just that. Childish, I suppose you could call it. But then she *was* childish. She liked playing games. Dressing up. Acting rôles. All that kind of thing.'

Outside the door now there was only silence. Jackson grunted and pushed his chair back a little. 'I doubt if they'll get that much out of the letter. You're going to have to get it all down in a statement, Mr Dobie. But you know that already.'

'Yes, *that* was childish, too. The confession, I mean. No way it could have been Kate, I'm not *that* short-sighted.'

'No,' Kate said, returning from the washbasin where she'd been scrubbing the blood off her hands. 'He's quite accurate at close range, I can vouch for that.'

'But then Wendy didn't know I'd rumbled her great impersonation act. Or more exactly, that the computer had. I'm glad,' Dobie said, 'it was Sammy who worked it all out and not me. It makes me feel he's evened the score a bit. I don't know why.'

He was aware that both Jackson and Kate were regarding him now with a certain curiosity. Or maybe it was concern.

'I think I'll go to bed now,' Dobie said.

* * *

Kate tucked him in nicely and stood back to look at him. She still had, he noticed, much the same expression on her face.

'You won't mind,' Dobie said, 'if I don't ask you to join me? Till a little later?'

'I don't see how I could possibly object to such a gentlemanly proposal. Or even,' Kate said, 'to its implications. Are you comfortable? . . . That's the main thing.'

'Yes, I am. I like it here. What I'll do is, I think I'll sell the flat.'

'Good,' Kate said. 'Then you can get that thing on to working out our income tax figures.'

Dobie wasn't too sure about that. It might be a little tricky. Something that he'd need to give a lot of thought to. Not now, of course. A little later.

No. *Much* later.

Dobie slept.

Paula Gosling

The Wychford Murders £3.99

By the author of *Monkey Puzzle* – winner of the Gold Dagger Award for the best crime novel of the year.

'Female, middle-aged, grabbed from behind, throat cut . . . No struggle, unconscious almost immediately, died in minutes from blood loss'

The gruesome murder of Beryl Tompkins brought Detective Chief Inspector Luke Abbott of the Regional Crime Squad back to Wychford, the sleepy little West Country village where he'd been born and raised.

For Abbot it was just another case, to be solved with as little fuss and as quickly as possible. But there were distractions. Jennifer Eames, whom he'd last seen twenty years before had grown into a beautiful woman. And Wychford too had changed. Behind the picture postcard prettiness it was seething with secret loves and hates, perversion, envy, jealousy and greed.

And now a second murder. Wyn Frenholm had nothing in common with Beryl Tompkins, except that her throat had also been horribly slashed. Either it was a copycat killing, or somewhere in Wychford a psychopath was loose . . .

In the classic tradition, *The Wychford Murders* is a brilliantly plotted, suspenseful whodunit with, in Luke Abbott, the latest in a long line of distinguished detectives.

Paula Gosling's *A Running Duck, The Zero Trap, The Woman in Red* and *Monkey Puzzle* are also available in Pan.

Loren D. Estleman
Silent Thunder £3.99

'It was the easiest case I'd ever solved. Now all I had to worry about was the one I'd been hired for . . .'

Doyle Thayer Junior died before they found Detroit's largest stash of illegal arms in his basement. But *a whole hour after* he beat up the wife accused of his murder.

Constance Thayer's excuse for killing her husband is simple self defence. Protecting herself from a man that more than one associate would have paid her to kill.

All private investigator Amos Walker is supposed to do is help prove the lady right. But digging for dirt on the city's most influential citizens is an art not a science. And it's an art that doesn't always go according to plan . . .

And like any art, it's open to interpretation . . .

'Loren D Estelman is the best and most original writer now working in the private eye tradition' JULIAN SYMONS, THE INDEPENDENT